J.B. WILLIAMS

Hobo Warrior Bunny: Episodes 01 - 04

First published by JB Writes Stuff 2024

Copyright © 2024 by J.B. Williams

All rights reserved. No part of this publication may be reproduced, stored or transmitted in any form or by any means, electronic, mechanical, photocopying, recording, scanning, or otherwise without written permission from the publisher. It is illegal to copy this book, post it to a website, or distribute it by any other means without permission.

This novel is entirely a work of fiction. The names, characters and incidents portrayed in it are the work of the author's imagination. Any resemblance to actual persons, living or dead, events or localities is entirely coincidental.

J.B. Williams asserts the moral right to be identified as the author of this work.

J.B. Williams has no responsibility for the persistence or accuracy of URLs for external or third-party Internet Websites referred to in this publication and does not guarantee that any content on such Websites is, or will remain, accurate or appropriate.

Designations used by companies to distinguish their products are often claimed as trademarks. All brand names and product names used in this book and on its cover are trade names, service marks, trademarks and registered trademarks of their respective owners. The publishers and the book are not associated with any product or vendor mentioned in this book. None of the companies referenced within the book have endorsed the book.

First edition

ISBN: 979-8-9895133-6-9

Editing by Stephen Zimmer
Cover art by JB Williams

This book was professionally typeset on Reedsy.
Find out more at reedsy.com

Contents

Acknowledgement v

I   When Fixers Come to Town

When Fixers Come to Town- 01	3
When Fixers Come to Town- 02	10
When Fixers Come to Town- 03	17
When Fixers Come to Town- 04	25
When Fixers Come to Town	37

II   A Bad Day

A Bad Day- 01	45
A Bad Day- 02	52
A Bad Day- 03	60
A Bad Day- 04	65
A Bad Day- 05	71

III   Relaxation

Relaxation- 01	79
Relaxation- 02	82
Relaxation- 03	90
Relaxation- 04	99

IV Bliss Town Reservoir

Bliss Town Reservoir- 01   113
Bliss Town Reservoir- 02   117
Bliss Town Reservoir- 03   124
Bliss Town Reservoir- 04   130
Bliss Town Reservoir- 05   134
Bliss Town Reservoir- 06   139

Acknowledgement

There are two people I'd like to acknowledge for helping to make this first batch of short stories possible.

- "Discover the Blue Hour" was very interested in the concept of *Hobo Warrior Bunny* and gave advice for the story. as well as read the original scripts. They were very helpful for the early stages of this story. They can be found at DTBH PODCAST - Werewolf Fiction & Popculture (discoveringthebluehour.com)
- Stephen Zimmer for turning a rough patch of work into a polished piece. He's been very helpful in making my writing better. He can be found Professional Editing and Publishing Services | Official Site of Author and Filmmaker Stephen Zimmer

I

When Fixers Come to Town

Jayson Hopper, the Hobo Warrior Bunny, and Lexia Hartwick, the Bazooka Bunny, fight for their lives against hired Fixers sent by the Mama Bear Syndicate.

When Fixers Come to Town- 01

Fifteen years ago, Bliss Town was a paradise.

Now it is Hell.

The once vibrant streets are now neglected and covered in filth, with cracked roads and dim lighting. Buildings made of colorful brick have lost their beauty, exposing their decay. Overlooking all this is a clock-shaped half-moon and a sky filled with shifting light blue cracks. And yet, four rabbit thugs armed with rifles remain unfazed, focused on the alley entrance while lukewarm rain patters against their bodies and the dead utopia.

The light from their van's headlights illuminates them and the rain, stretching their shadows across the grungy cement.

The leader of the group, a pale-brown rabbit with slick dark hair and dark eyes takes a deep breath and looks at his wristwatch, his face scrunched and shoulders tight. This is Rolland Longstaff, and he would rather be playing One-O than getting soggy.

"Two more minutes and we're gone," says Rolland.

And as if the universe heard him, a rumbling and sputtering engine catches their ears. A small, rundown vehicle with patches of rust turns into the alley, shining its dim lights on Rolland's group.

The vehicle crawls towards them, its exhaust sounding like gunshots. Its brakes screech and it stops a few feet away from the thugs.

The beat-up car creaks open, and two thin, unkempt rabbits covered in grease and reeking of old cheese stumble out. They are Kerry Thatcher and Jude Caden; walking clichés of addicts that infuriate Rolland but also bring him the money to make his weekly quota, which in turn makes him happy since it keeps him from getting stuffed in an acid barrel. So, it balances out.

"Wassup, you got the stuff 'cuz I got the money and I need the Reel. Like bad, man. Real bad," says Kerry.

Jude nods spastically. "Yeah. Same here. Same here. I got money, too. I need Reel Sight real bad."

Rolland looks at his partner, an all-black rabbit whose brown eyes bring the only different shade to him. "Get it out."

The black rabbit, Dacre Ridge, goes into the van, and the two other thugs pace around, clutching their weapons tight and shivering in the rain as they scan the area for trouble. The first one is Cyrus Clarkson; he has mostly white fur with dark hair, but his ears, cheeks, and the area around his eyes are covered in black fur. The other one is Shae Ray, who also has mostly white fur; but his muzzle and ears are covered in brown fur, and his hair **used to be** brown, but this week he dyed it a delightful shade of gold.

But with Dacre distracted by rummaging through the van, Rolland scrutinizing Kerry and Jude, Kerry and Jude being unfocused messes, and Cyrus and Shae looking everywhere but up, they fail to notice a rabbit-shaped silhouette on the roof. The shadow slides out of sight when Shae turns to their direction, **almost** looking up.

Finally, after several long seconds of rummaging, Dacre approaches Rolland with a locked metal tin.

"About time," says Rolland to Dacre, then to Kerry and Jude, "Show us the money."

"Right... Money. Money," mutters Kerry.

Kerry and Jude pull out zip-lock bags full of wadded bills and old coins, and Rolland sneers.

"You serious?" he says.

"It's all we have," says Jude.

Rolland looks at Dacre. "Count them."

Dacre roughly grabs the bags, plops them on the hood of the rundown car and counts, uncaring of the currency getting wet from the falling rain. As he counts, Rolland keeps his eyes on the drug addicts, and Cyrus and Shae continue pacing around with minimal enthusiasm.

"One's got twenty bucks and fifteen cents. The other has thirty-three bucks and five cents," says Dacre.

Rolland nods with puckered lips. "Impressive. Combined, you get one pill."

Kerry steps forward aggressively, causing Rolland to snap up his rifle, which brings the others to aim their weapons at the two addicts. Kerry and Jude step back with their hands raised and their bodies shivering.

"Come on, man. Those pills ain't worth that much," says Kerry.

"Mama Bear is adjusting the prices to account for inflation," says Rolland.

"Ain't no way they're worth forty bucks each!"

"It's fifty bucks a pill. Now you either get one pill, or you drive off."

Kerry looks at Jude. They nod, return the money to their bags, and slowly drive away in reverse. Rolland scrunches his brow and flips the safety off his rifle, and the others ready themselves.

The vehicle keeps reversing until it is at the edge of the alley. Then the engine revs with sputters and pops, and the tires squeal as they zoom towards the thugs, kicking up the water as they go.

Rolland's group scatters, and the addicts hit the van. Glass and headlight shatters, and the thugs shoot at the car, piercing its hood and destroying its windshield.

Kerry and Jude duck down. Their seats are decimated by the gunfire and the rear view window pops loose as smoke rises from the engine.

And while Rolland's group is distracted, a blur leaps from the rooftop and kicks Shae into the van.

Shae crumbles to the ground, creating a small splash, and the remaining thugs snap around as mysterious figure rolls to his feet, his details shrouded by the night. He draws a wooden sword that glows in the dark; white dots and swirling shades of blue and brown cover it, like a galaxy trapped in wood. And Rolland's group gets a mixture of fear and annoyance.

"Ah, shit. It's the Hobo Warrior Bunny!" says Cyrus.

"You got to be freaking kidding me," says Dacre.

"Die, Hobo!" screams Rolland.

The Hobo Warrior tightens his grip on his odd weapon, creating a faint blue aura that surrounds him. He lunges forward in a burst of intense speed and whacks the guns and thugs with his wooden weapon.

Muzzle flashes light up pockets of the dark alley, and the cracks of gunfire echo in the sleeping town. But inside the aura, the thugs are slowed by one second, giving the Hobo Warrior Bunny more than enough leverage to unleash his skills against them.

The strikes from his weapon knock their aim off, and he uses great speed to deflect and counter punches, kicks, or clubbing attempts. As the fight carries on, Jude takes a couple of tins that fell to the ground and jumps back in his car.

"Go! Go! Go!" orders Jude.

Kerry speeds backwards before Jude can close the door, fishtails in the road, and drives off, tires squealing and exhaust and smoke rolling in the rainy air.

In the midst of the chaos, the Hobo Warrior Bunny overpowers Dacre and delivers a final blow to Cyrus that leaves him limp on the ground. As he turns his attention towards Rolland, the thug aims his rifle at the Hobo's head.

Rolland pulls the trigger, but the rifle is pushed up with one hand and the Hobo rams his weapon into the thug's gut, dropping him to his knees and making him wheeze for air.

Immediately after, a rocket strikes the van.

The resulting explosion launches the pair into the brick wall. They crumble into a muddy puddle with the wooden weapon falling out of the Hobo Warrior Bunny's grip, causing the aura to disperse. The two cough and sputter, and they get on their knees, but before Rolland can recover, the Hobo Warrior slams his head against the brick wall.

Rolland goes limp, and the Hobo Warrior winces while using the wall to help him stand. The fire's light illuminates him, revealing him to be a male white rabbit in his mid-twenties, a thick, brown tuft of fur on his head, and bright blue eyes weighed down with black bags. His ratty clothing is colored in shades of blue, with a ratty, blue, handwoven scarf around his neck. To the thugs of the Mama Bear Syndicate, he is the Hobo Warrior Bunny. But to his associates, he is Jayson Hopper.

Jayson looks across the street and sees a silhouette of a rabbit figure on the rooftop holding a bulky, homemade bazooka.

Jayson's eyes narrow and the figure runs away. He snatches his weapon off the ground, slips it into a junker-sheath on his hip, and runs across the street while sirens accompanied by police lights approach in the distance.

Jayson jumps on top of a parked car and uses it to give him a boost for his next jump, bringing him to grab a windowsill, and he quickly climbs to the roof.

Once Jayson reaches the roof, he sees the maniac with the bazooka leaping to another building. He growls irritably and continues the chase, skillfully jumping from rooftop to rooftop.

Despite the head start of the menace, Jayson is able to quickly catch up. He runs faster, jumps faster and longer than his target, and when he reaches them, he takes a flying leap and makes the tackle.

They roll across the rooftop and Jayson is kicked away. He bounces back to his feet and finds the barrel of the bazooka pointed at his face.

Behind the homemade bazooka is the bane of his existence; the menace of all menaces; the turd in the punch bowl: Bazooka Bunny.

Her name is Lexia Hartwick, and she's the same age as Jayson, but a genetic anomaly. Half-hare, half-harlequin rabbit, she towers over everyone in Bliss Town with her muscular frame. She has a white left side and a brown right side, her ears are striped brown and white, and she wears a homemade armored outfit with a knee length, heavy gray fabric skirt.

"Your weapon isn't loaded, **Lexia**," says Jayson.

Lexia snaps her bazooka down on Jayson's head like a club, but he swiftly blocks it with his cosmic weapon, bringing the rain to briefly slow down around him as its light blue aura flickers in and out of existence.

"There's more than one way to use a bazooka, **Jayson**," sneers Lexia.

Jayson shoves the bazooka away, and Lexia swiftly draws a pistol. Jayson grabs it and forces it down. The pistol goes off, striking near his foot.

Jayson elbows Lexia in the jaw and disarms her. She stumbles and Jayson throws the pistol away, fuming.

"What's wrong with you! Are you trying to kill me!" says Jayson.

Lexia snaps up with a maniacal grin, her bazooka now loaded and aimed at Jayson.

"Yes!" yells Lexia.

Lexia fires her bazooka and Jayson dodges the strike, but the resulting explosion causes their corner of the building to collapse. They tumble together, with burning debris raining down and dust rolling into the alley.

As they fall, Jayson uses Lexia as a shield and rams her into the neighboring brick wall with a winged DNA strand painted on it. Bricks break upon impact, and they crash into the dirty alley flooded with filthy water. When they stagger up, Lexia rams Jayson into a dumpster and draws a knife.

She delivers swift, vicious swipes, but Jayson evades and deflects most of them with his wooden sword, getting very few cuts, despite Lexia and the rain slowing down around him.

Jayson manages to disarm Lexia after a few swipes, but she disarms him immediately after and kicks his weapon away. Then the pair exchange swift, sharp blows in hand-to-hand combat.

They are vicious with each other. Punching, kicking, ramming, tackling, rolling over each other, biting, clawing, cursing, and screaming profanity and insults, all while getting soaked in the filthy alley water.

The two rivals are so engrossed in their duel to the death that they do not notice a figure swooping down and approaching them with heavy steps.

Only when they are choking each other do they realize that someone is watching them. They pause, slowly look up, and are yanked to their knees and have their heads slammed together.

They fall on their butts and rub their heads while a middle-aged, male bald eagle, ragged with age and broken dreams, stands above them. He is dressed like a rugged traveler and is absolutely tired of their nonsense. This is Derrick Marlow.

With them discombobulated, Derrick grabs Lexia's bazooka and glares at the two rabbits.

"Get up and meet me at my nest," orders Derrick.

Then he flies away, and Lexia and Jayson watch him go, still tenderly rubbing their heads. Their rubbing gradually stops, and they glare at each other with the clock-styled moon and the cracks in the night sky providing some light for them.

They get up and momentarily lean against each other, but the connection is used by both of them to bounce away and use the dumpster or brick wall for support. Several seconds of recuperation pass, and they pull away from their support, with Lexia putting her hands on her hips to glare at Jayson while he picks up his cosmic-wood sword.

"How come he didn't take your stupid stick?" asks Lexia.

Jayson wipes his weapon with his sleeve, despite him being soaked and the rain still drizzling.

"Maybe because my **cosmic** stick doesn't blow up stuff," says Jayson. He sheathes his weapon and gestures for Lexia to lead. "By the way, ladies first."

Lexia scoffs and walks forward, passing Jayson with heavy steps. "I was going to go first, anyway."

"Good. I don't trust you being behind me," says Jayson.

"Ha!" blurts Lexia obnoxiously, and she inspects her hand smugly as she continues forward, putting a little sway in her steps as rainwater rolls off her. "As if that's supposed to hurt my feelings. Me being in front is actually a good thing for you because you are too weak to do anything to me! Even with low-blow sneak attacks. Which means that the menaces of society are scared away from us with me leading the way."

When Lexia doesn't hear a retort, she turns around and sees Jayson is gone, and she frowns.

"Wow... What a prick."

When Fixers Come to Town- 02

The rain has gradually ceased during Jayson's trek to Derrick's nest, passing a decaying sign with a 1950s-style motif of a young and happy eagle family on a porch, overlooking the lush, expansive forest. Now the colors of the sign have faded, exposed wood is splintering, and failing lights cast a dim glow on the words, "*Welcome to the Eagle Enclave. Where your family tree will be problem free!*"

The soggy ground squishes underneath Jayson's boots (held together by duct tape), with some water seeping through to soak his scrappy socks. The light from the moon and cracked sky gives him enough guidance to navigate the forest of a variety of tree breeds and sizes, with many of them being young. The older trees that remain healthy have houses built on them, held up by sturdy branches and poles with their utilities snaking down the host tree. These elevated homes also provide some light through their windows and porch doors. Trees that have died remain empty, with some having abandoned houses stuck on them, or, in a couple of bad cases, the houses fell to the ground, leaving them as shattered messes of wood and glass consumed by nature.

As Jayson walks through the forest, he passes a gutted tank here, a crashed plane there, a collapsed pill box in the distance, and a destroyed wall that has been reclaimed by the wilderness. He's certain he's walking on graves, too, even though he hasn't seen any skeletons, but it doesn't shake the feeling off.

Jayson exits the forest and enters a clearing of mostly dead trees and lots of craters that have been reclaimed by grass or turned into miniature swamps. Some of the dead trees have been splintered to pieces, and others have collapsed to their sides. Yet despite this, twigs of new life have managed to sprout in the desolation, and off in the distance is a large, old tree with a circular house built high into it, isolated from the other homes in the Eagle Enclave.

A flicker of a smile graces Jayson's lips and he trudges forward. When he gets to his destination, he uses branches and thick, sturdy bark to climb. After ascending four dozen feet, he pulls himself over a railing and lands on the house porch. He takes a moment to recollect his breath and wipes his hands on his pants.

Nearby is Derrick, sitting on a chair with a scoped rifle on a swivel platform and a patio umbrella fixed above him. He has a cigarette in his beak, and next to him is Lexia's bazooka and a coffee machine plugged to an outside outlet.

"Where's Lexia?" asks Derrick.

"She's on her way," replies Jayson.

Derrick grunts and uses his foot to nudge a dry crate to Jayson.

"Have a seat," says Derrick.

Jayson sits on the crate and puts his wooden sword between his legs. He and Derrick quietly watch the moon, the cracks in the sky, the mountains, and the burning smoke from Bliss Town. There are faint sirens in the distance, and Derrick leans forward and peers through his scope.

"Here she comes," says Derrick.

Jayson and Derrick wait in silence, and a few minutes later, Lexia's grunts and angry mutters and ruffling leaves get louder as she climbs the tree. Moments later, Lexia's brown hand rises above the railing, grips it hard, followed by her white hand doing the same thing. Lexia pulls herself up, struggling and sweating. She flops over the railing and lands on her back, panting heavily.

Jayson and Derrick stare at Lexia, and she rolls on her hands and knees and glares at Jayson, her arms quivering and sweat rolling off her face.

"You..." wheezes Lexia.

"Yes?" says Jayson.

"YOU!"

"Yes?"

"You left me!"

"You shot a rocket at me. Twice."

Lexia points at Derrick. "And you stole my bazooka!"

Derrick points at her weapon. "It's right there."

Lexia gets up on wobbly legs, but before she can grab her weapon, Derrick holds up his talon.

"Hold on. Before you get your tool back, you mind explaining why you two were butting heads again?" says Derrick.

"She shot a rocket at me," says Jayson.

"You were in the way," says Lexia.

"I was there first!"

"No, I was! This whole town is my territory and you're the one encroaching on my turf!"

"I'm talking about the alley, not the town."

"The alley is part of the town!"

"This town is big enough for the two of us."

"NO, IT'S NOT! FIND YOUR OWN TOWN TO LIBERATE, HOBO!"

Jayson jabs his thumb at Lexia as he looks at Derrick.

"See what I have to deal with?" says Jayson.

Derrick sighs heavily and rubs his brow. "Lexia, we've been over this. Jayson grew up here. This is his home as much as yours. You need to share this town with him."

Jayson smiles smugly at Lexia.

"Bull crap," snaps Lexia. "I've never seen him before. And I've never left this place."

"Check the Bliss Town Academy Yearbook. I'm in there," says Jayson.

"No, you aren't," says Lexia.

Jayson frowns and grips his cosmic weapon tight.

"Lexia, if you want to beat Mama Bear, then you have to cooperate with him," says Derrick. "And I have an idea that will help you two deal with your rivalry while being a thorn in Mama Bear's side. Come inside."

Derrick tosses his cigarette over the porch, removes his rifle from the stand, and escorts Jayson and Lexia inside.

The interior of Derrick's nest is a liminal space; brightly lit, but mostly empty. The walls are blank in a yellow drab, and doors are locked with padlocks and wood planks nailed over them. The only areas accessible are the kitchen, dining room, living room, and bathroom. The kitchen and dining room are spartan, and in the living room is a sofa, a coffee table, a makeshift nest made of pillows, cushions, and blankets, and an entertainment center that doubles as a dresser. There are shelves that are full of painted figurines of grimdark, far-future sci-fi warriors, with more boxes and paint sets stacked on top of each other; and there is a broken grandfather clock tipped on its side in the back.

Lastly, there is a whiteboard on a rolling stand with a map of Bliss Town drawn on it. The map is split down the middle. The left half is marked with a cartoony head of Lexia. The right side is marked with a cartoony head of Jayson. The line goes straight down Main Street, and curves over to the mountainous area. The *Bliss Town Mall, Sam & Mann Super Market, Cindy's Cinema,* and the *Community Center* are marked as neutral zones.

"Seeing as how you two can't get along, I'll have to give you two your own territory so you can do your work without causing too much damage," says Derrick as he pulls the map to the dining room.

With that statement, Jayson looks at Lexia, and she turns her nose up. As they do this, Derrick goes to the dining table, grabs two marked maps, and gives them to the pair.

"Lexia, you have the West Side. Jayson has the East Side," says Derrick.

Jayson and Lexia inspect their maps for a few seconds before Jayson looks at Derrick quizzically.

"Why does Lexia get Arty's Arcade?" asks Jayson.

"Why do you care? You can't afford it," says Lexia. Then she squints at her map. "Hey, wait a minute. Your side has Samantha's Spa! Derrick, you suck at making borders!"

Derrick casually lights a new cigarette.

"I'll tell you what, you can go to the spa, and in exchange, you let me go to the arcade," says Jayson.

"Fine. But you are only allowed on my side when I take spa days. They are every Sunday, from noon to three," says Lexia.

"Fine by me." Jayson looks at his map again. "You have The Crystal Plate on your side."

"I know for a fact you can't afford The Crystal Plate," says Lexia.

"Of course not. But their trash is really good. You have to let me over there. At least on Fridays and Saturdays."

Lexia wrinkles her nose. "And what could you possibly offer me in exchange for that?"

"Uh... Taco King?" offers Jayson.

"No deal."

"Taco King has amazing deals on Fridays and Saturdays. And their King Don burritos are criminally good."

"Maybe if I wanted to explosively lose weight, I would take up your offer, but I happen to value my amazing physique and intestines."

Jayson rolls his eyes. "Give me a break. That's just a crappy rumor. I've never had any 'explosive weight loss' incidents from Taco King."

"That's because you got the stomach from Hell. Literally nothing makes you sick," claims Lexia.

"Are you two done?" says Derrick.

"We're still negotiating," says Jayson.

Lexia folds up her map and stuffs it against her belt. "Negotiations are over."

"Great. Now both of you get out and if I see you two trying to kill each other again I'm going to be very angry with you," says Derrick.

"Oooh... Spooky threat," says Lexia while waving her fingers.

The room dims and Derrick's eyes glow bright red as he glares at the two rabbits. The two recoil, with Lexia holding Jayson in front of her and cringing with drooped ears.

"I mean... Have a good night?" says Lexia.

Next thing Jayson and Lexia know, they are being shoved outside, with Lexia holding her bazooka tightly against her chest. The door slams shut behind them, making them flinch, and after a couple seconds of stillness, Jayson relaxes with heavy breath, and he walks to the railing.

"Smooth," says Jayson.

Lexia walks after him while clipping her bazooka to her back. "Well, none of this would have happened if you didn't get in my way."

"Bull."

"No bull. You getting in my way all the time is causing friction, which is leading to stress, which is leading to mental problems."

Jayson grips the railing and looks at Lexia, eyes heavy and lips tight with a frown, while the beast masquerading as a female goes next to him.

"Have you tried being a regular hobo? You know, like the ones that live in homeless shelters with a warm bed, warm food, showers, job placement programs? Bliss Town doesn't have them, but there's a place one hundred miles from here that does," says Lexia. She leans against the railing and flashes a smile. "I can even give you a ride there, free of charge."

"No," says Jayson.

Lexia's smile drops, and Jayson climbs over the railing. He expertly climbs down using the tree branches and bark. After a few seconds, Lexia fumbles her way after him, snapping branches, breaking bark, and grumbling about Derrick needing to install a ladder.

"You know, Lexia, instead of blaming me for your woes, maybe you should look at yourself and not shoot rockets at everything. Or everyone. Specifically, me," says Jayson.

Lexia makes a poor imitation of Jayson. "Oh, mer gersh, maybe you shouldn't be a meanie and blow-up pea-pul. Nananana—"

Suddenly Lexia's branch snaps and she lurches forward.

"OH SHIT!" screams Lexia.

Lexia tumbles down, bouncing off branches and falling past Jayson, who rolls his eyes and continues downward with great skill. When he reaches the last branch, he jumps off and lands next to Lexia, who is face-first in the soggy ground, surrounded by leaves and broken branches.

"You okay?" asks Jayson.

Lexia's groan is muffled in the muddy mulch. "Buzz off."

"Sure thing."

Jayson pats Lexia's head and walks away, and Lexia remains in the mulch, fuming.

"Have a good night," says Jayson while giving her a half-hearted wave.

Lexia growls. "You too... Prick."

Jayson smiles and keeps walking. It is a lovely way to end the night.

When Fixers Come to Town- 03

Dawn has come, and bugs and small songbirds have come out to fill the air with their buzzes and calls. The bronze, orange, and yellow hues of the sky are warped by the extensive cracks reaching over the horizon. The light shines on an abandoned factory. Its brick and metal structures have crumbled and rusted with plants overtaking it, and what hasn't been reclaimed by nature has been covered with graffiti; some demonic, some vulgar, and some professing love to people doomed to heartbreak. The largest one is of a crowd of people trying to flee a city while being dissolved by a green cloud.

Next to the factory's caved in visitor center is Jude and Kerry's car. The hood has blackened, engine fluids have stained the ground beneath, and rainwater has seeped into the wrecked seats. The passenger door is open, and Jude is slumped against the tire, eyes dim and mouth filled with bloody foam.

Inside the car is Kerry, twitching and giggling. His hands quiver as he opens the tin. It is mostly empty now, but a few blue pills remain. He pops one in his mouth and swallows it dry; soon after, his crusty red eyes widen, and his pupils dilate.

The world becomes brighter and warps. It glitters with colorful swirls rising around him as plants turn to pulsing colors and the old facility changes to colorful bricks with ghostly butterflies and shifting orbs floating around.

"Come home, Kerry," says an orb, its voice a soothing whisper in his ears.

Multiple butterflies circle Kerry.

"Come see with us," they say over each other. "Jude is here. He sees with us."

"Where is Jude?" wonders Kerry, his eyes following the butterflies and orbs.

"Here I am!" says Jude.

Kerry looks to the side and sees a wide variety of colorful orbs and butterflies congregate together to make a male figure. It doesn't look like Jude, but it has his voice, so it must be Jude, and it holds out its hand to him.

"Come see with me," says Jude.

Kerry smiles with tears in his eyes, and sweat rolls down his head, unaware of a feminine angelic figure made from butterflies and swirling mist approaching him from around the corner. As the figure approaches, Kerry holds out his hand to the butterflies and orbs in front of him, and the figure's hand stretches into the car.

"Come see with me," says Jude.

A sudden rapping on Kerry's door causes his ears to perk, and he turns his head to see a mass made of butterflies and blotches of light and darkness rolling over each other.

"Whoa... Are you an angel?" asks Kerry.

Then everything goes dark.

****

Three suppressed gunshots and shattering glass echoes in the vicinity, and three more suppressed gunshots follows soon after. The interior of the car is splashed with blood, and Kerry is slumped awkwardly in his seat with one hole in his head and two in his chest. Jude has the same pattern.

As the blood soaks into the seat and ground, a slender prairie rattlesnake rummages through the vehicle. She has golden hair, red eyes, and orange scales with brown spots on her body, and a brown stripe leading from her forehead, covering her muzzle, and going down her neck. She is dressed as a 1920s mobster with a hat and long coat and has a suppressed pistol in her holster, a Thompson rifle on her back, and snazzy polished black shoes. It doesn't take her long to find the tin of Reel Sight, but she frowns when she finds only two of the blue pills remaining. She stuffs the tin in her pocket and retrieves a radio clipped to her belt.

"Mortimer, this is Claribel, I found the thieves and the product. But the thieves helped themselves to a lot of Reel Sight," says the snake, Claribel Belle Blair, with a slight South Welsh accent.

Her radio crackles, and a lackadaisical voice breaks through.

"That's a shame. I talked to Rolland and Dacre, and they told me that they lost the stuff after they were attacked by the Hobo Warrior Bunny," says Mortimer Walters.

Claribel scoffs. "Him again, huh?"

****

Inside a dirty hotel room, where the nasty windows have given the light a brown tint, is Mortimer Walters. He is a male fox with his right side scarred and his right ear mangled, and lush dark hair styled in a comb over. He is wearing a magician outfit, and his eyes are locked on a particular figure across the street. One hand is lightly holding the curtain, while the other holds his radio.

On his bed is a large collection of crushed *Roadrunner Rampage* energy drink cans, ranging from apple to bubblegum, and kiwi to strawberry, pumpkin spice to gape, and one can chocolate coffee flavored. There is also a metal case with a lock and a winged DNA strand. The case is dented, and the symbol has faded and chipped in spots.

"Yeah. They also said Bazooka Bunny struck them and tried to kill the Hobo along with them," says Mortimer.

"I see... Well, as much fun as it will be to take care of them now, I spent all night looking for this stupid car and I have other things I need to do today. We can deal with those two troublemakers together when we make a good plan," says Claribel over the radio.

"I'd rather take care of them now. The sooner the better. But if you want to relax, go ahead. I'll still split the money with you when I kill both of them."

"Thanks. I still need to check in to the safehouse. You need to check in too, so that way we can plan things."

"Yeah, yeah, sure, whatever. I'll see you when I see you. Over and out," says Mortimer.

He clicks off his radio and keeps his focus on Jayson Hopper, who is sitting on a bench, slouched from exhaustion, with a cup in hand and a sign that says: "**DOWN ON LUCK. ANYTHING HELPS.**"

Nobody pays attention to him. And he doesn't notice Mortimer staring at him from a dirty window in the third story of the hotel across the street. Seeing the Hobo's filthy and starved state brings Mortimer to wonder how the twig has managed to cause so many problems.

And while Mortimer watches Jayson, a tall ram with red and white fur, bright blue eyes, wearing a tailored suit and golfer's cap stops to give Jayson a few dollars. Nothing remarkable.

****

Outside, in the beautiful cool morning with sunlight shining down, Jayson is caught by surprise by the large sum of bills tossed in his cup. He looks up, curious about the source of generosity, and sees a tall ram in a nice suit.

"There you go, ole chap. Get yourself some protein. You need it," says the Tall Ram.

"Thank you, sir," says Jayson.

"No. Thank you."

Jayson raises a brow and the Tall Ram walks away, whistling. The stranger rounds the corner, and Jayson shrugs and leaves his spot to go to a nearby food cart for a breakfast burrito. After buying one, Jayson sits down on his bench and watches the cars pass by. But as the commuters go about their business, Jayson notices Lexia sitting on a raised concrete bed, staring at him with a tight frown and eyes smoldering.

Cars pass by and the two keep eye contact. No one cares that Lexia is wearing her armor and has a bazooka on her back (or pistols or knives on her belt) or that Jayson has an odd-looking piece of wood in his possession.

Jayson's heavy blue eyes drift around to look at something else, but they find their way back to Lexia.

As they stare at each other, a fox wearing a magician outfit and a raccoon mask arrives with a wrapped case and a small cart. He sets up shop near Jayson and starts making balloon figures. This draws children and parents out from the ether.

After a few more cars pass, Lexia puts her hands to her mouth and screams, "I'M COMING OVER! DO NOT ASSAULT ME!"

Jayson mimics Lexia. "YOU SHOT ME WITH A ROCKET!"

"YOU STARTED IT!"

"DID NOT!"

"DID TOO!"

"Just shut up and cross the road!" shouts a random guy down the sidewalk. Lexia glares at him. "HEY, BUZZ OFF!"

"No, you."

Lexia huffs and crosses the street, ignoring the cars screeching to a stop and honking. Jayson stares at her with a twitching eye. When she reaches the other side, she stands next to him, puts her arm over his shoulder and leans against him.

"Listen, I know we got off on the wrong foot, but I think we can use a break from hostilities for the day," says Lexia.

"We've been on the wrong foot since day one," says Jayson.

"How's the saying go? Every day is a new day, so technically every day is day one, and the stress of this rivalry is really bad for us and—"

"You want to go to Samantha's Spa."

"Yes, I do. I'm bored and there's no criminals for me to blow you up with."

"I don't know. We had our agreement and it's not Sunday."

"Jayson, please don't be a pill. I did not sleep good at all and—"

Jayson holds up his hand. "Stop! Don't..." He sighs heavily and reluctantly says, "I'll let you have the spa only on the condition that I get to go to Arty's Arcade."

Lexia seethes and rubs her hair, and Jayson stares at her with a small smile twitching on his lips.

"Well, Lexia?" says Jayson.

"Fine. I guess I'll let you go to Arty's Arcade," says Lexia.

Jayson grins, slaps Lexia's arm, and hops away.

"Great! Enjoy getting pampered with sand," says Jayson.

Lexia growls and yells after him, "I will! And that **mud** is a hundred times better than the dirt you sleep in!"

"Whatever you say, sand lover!" hollers Jayson.

Lexia huffs and walks away; and Mortimer makes one more balloon in the shape of a snake. He bows theatrically to the impressed crowd of children and walks after Jayson with his metal case, leaving all his balloon stuff behind. Which is raided by the children.

****

On the outskirts of Bliss Town is a rundown house. The colors have faded, the chimney is held in place with metal bands, and the warped glass and door frame is protected by a layer of razor wire. Nearby is a small playground with a bent swing set, a broken slide, and weeds conquering a sandbox.

Inside, the rundown house is not much better. The lights vary from dim to bright, the wallpaper is peeling, the paint is stained, and the former gray carpet has blotches of odd colors.

In the living room, Rolland, Dacre, Cyrus, and Shae are playing One-O with their weapons laying nearby. They are sitting on the floor, using filthy couch cushions as seats while the TV is on mute and displaying a male squirrel in a nice suit getting a lighthearted interview from a female rabbit news anchor.

The front metal door opens, spilling natural light into the room, and Claribel Belle Blair enters, pulling a large rolling suitcase that has another suitcase strapped on top of it.

Rolland's group snaps their weapons to Claribel, and her steps are slow and steady as she walks in, holding back a grimace as the carpet squelches and oozes an odd green puss under her polished shoes.

Both sides stare at each other while Claribel uses her tail to close the door, but while she is tired and somewhat relieved to have found the safehouse, Rolland's group is shocked at what they are seeing.

"Dude... Is that a snake?" asks Dacre.

"I think that's a snake," says Cyrus.

"Where did she come from?" wonders Shae.

"Excuse me, miss, do you mind telling us who you are and why you're here?" says Rolland.

"Claribel Belle Blair. Mama Bear sent me here," says Claribel. "Where's Mortimer?"

"Mama Bear didn't say you were a snake," says Rolland.

"Is that going to be a problem?"

Rolland's group stares at Claribel, and she looks at them. Her eyes slowly narrow and her tail rattles as she puts her hand on her pistol holster. Several seconds of heavy heartbeats pass before Rolland shrugs and looks at his cards.

"Nah. We'll be fine. Do you want to play One-O?" asks Rolland.

"No. But I want to know where Mortimer is," says Claribel.

"The fox with the ugly face?"

Claribel's tail rattles again.

"Yeah, he showed up at midnight and set up his room," continues Rolland. "Then he took all of our energy drinks and left. Haven't seen him since."

Claribel takes a moment to process this, and then she thanks Rolland and walks past the group, her grip on her gear tight.

She goes down a hallway, leading to a set of stairs, and she is careful with her load, so it doesn't jerk around too much as she climbs the stairs.

"Dude, she dresses like one of those nerds at a convention," says Dacre. He's trying to be quiet, but he is still speaking loud enough for Claribel to hear.

"Don't insult the snake. She'll bite you if you get her mad," says Cyrus.

"Or choke you out with that tail. Which I wouldn't mind," says Shae.

"Just play your cards," says Rolland.

Claribel's posture drops slightly, and when she gets up the stairs, she goes down the hallway until she reaches her room, which is marked with a sign that reads, "*Reserved for Claribel.*"

Claribel opens the door and enters a good-sized room with a simple bedroom set. She closes and locks the door, then places her suitcases on the bed. After that, she opens the top suitcase and pulls out a bulky desktop computer with a green illuminated keyboard and mouse, and a fluffy headset. She sets up all this on the desk. After that, she opens the larger suitcase and removes her collection of rifles, pistols, and ammunition, all of which are wrapped in felt blankets and bubble wrap.

"Heeeey Claaaaair – how's it going?" asks Mortimer over the radio, his tone light and teasing.

Claribel hisses and pulls her radio off her belt.

"You didn't tell me you were already here," says Claribel.

"I thought it was obvious when I said I talked to Rolland," says Mortimer.

"You were supposed to meet me at the safehouse so we could handle this together."

"I wanted to go together, but you said you had other things to do before I left."

"I know, but you could have waited at the house so we could plan things together."

"Plan what? How to kill a hobo and an Amazonian LARPer? Please, this job will be easy. Not much planning is needed."

Claribel sits hard on the bed.

"Speaking of hobo and LARPer, the Hobo Warrior Bunny and Bazooka Bunny suck at hiding," continues Mortimer. "I'm trailing the Hobo now, but I overheard the Bazooka Bunny say she was going to Samantha's Spa."

"Thanks. I'll take care of her," says Claribel, her tone dejected.

"Dinner after?"

Claribel shakes her head. "No. I still got stuff to do. I'll see you when the job is done."

Claribel drops her radio on the bed and checks her equipment. Seeing everything is in order, she takes a deep breath and exits the room.

When Fixers Come to Town- 04

A bell above the entrance of Samantha's Spa dings with a delightful charm. The lobby is brightly lit, with pink and fluffy furniture, healthy plants, up-to-date magazines, and a TV displaying a home improvement show. The lobby is populated with lots of female rabbits of various shapes, sizes, and colors waiting in comfy chairs, and Lexia couldn't be happier being in such a wonderful place.

With a bright smile and small hops, Lexia (dressed casually in jeans and a sleeveless shirt) goes to the counter. She rings the bell and coolly leans against the polished wood as she inspects her fingers. A moment later, the secretary approaches with a clipboard and pen. The secretary is a female lop-eared rabbit with white fur, long brown ears, curly black hair, and a permanent bored expression that matches her grayish blue eyes. Her name is Mariana Cross, and she wants to go home.

"The usual?" asks Mariana.

"The usual," replies Lexia.

"Cash?"

"Cash."

"Now?"

Lexia takes out a crumpled wad of bills and drops them on the counter. "Now."

Mariana's expression remains unchanged as she stiffly grabs the money and drags it off the counter without looking away from Lexia's eyes. Once she has the money secured in the drawer, Mariana drops a ticket in front of Lexia and writes her name on the clipboard.

"You'll be number seventeen," says Mariana.

"What happened to 'now?'" asks Lexia.

Mariana stares at Lexia, and Lexia snatches the ticket off the counter.

"Actually, never mind. I'll wait. I like waiting. I'll wait right over here. Patiently."

Lexia sits next to the TV and stretches out her legs, hands folded on her lap, and her smile strained. Her thumbs twirl against each other, and her eyes dart around before looking at the rabbit next to her. She is a pampered, skinny, white lop-eared rabbit with long blonde hair and hazel eyes, slightly older than her and Jayson, and she is reading a magazine about popsicle stick crafts.

"Patience is my middle name, you know," says Lexia.

"Your mom says its Gertrude," says the skinny rabbit without looking up.

"Lies and deceit! ... I changed it to Xenia... Court pending approval."

"Hmhm," hums the rabbit, flipping the page.

"Number seven," calls Mariana.

Lexia gasps and perks, and Mariana looks at her.

"*Just* number seven. Vanessa McNessa," says Mariana.

Lexia slouches, and the pampered rabbit puts the magazine on the table next to her and walks away.

"Say hi to your mom for me," says Vanessa McNessa.

"Uh huh, sure. Totally," grumbles Lexia, lips twisted to a pout and her legs stretched out.

****

On the streets of Bliss Town, Claribel is studying her copy of the local map while chugging a *Road Runner Rampage* energy drink. It tastes like kiwi, and its effects have been disappointingly mediocre.

Her Stetson hat protects her eyes from the sun, and people slow their walks as they give a wide berth to pass her while giving her cautious looks. Even a police car passing by slows to a crawl so the cops can inspect her from a distance.

Claribel is not bothered by their antics. After all, it is not often a snake makes an appearance, much less a snake with a Thompson gun who looks like they crawled out of a 1920s mobster den. No, her annoyance is with the map.

"Where the hell is Samantha's Spa?" wonders Claribel, her hand crushing the now-empty energy can.

A shadow looms over Claribel, and she stiffens and looks behind her to see the Tall Ram reading over her shoulder. This causes her tail to rattle.

"Can I help you?" asks Claribel.

The Tall Ram points down the road.

"Miss, I believe the Spa is down that way," he says.

Claribel looks down the road, then at the map.

"It won't be on that map. Your map is ten years old, and Samantha's Spa is five years old." The Tall Ram reaches into his coat pocket and gives her a neatly folded map. "Here, have mine instead. It was printed earlier this year."

Claribel hesitantly takes the map. "Thanks...?"

"No problem," says the Tall Ram. He pulls out an eighty gram protein bar and starts eating. "Enjoy your day at the spa. You look like you need it."

Claribel is speechless about this claim, so rather than trying to find words, she just leaves. Her steps are quick, and the pedestrians moving out of her way are quicker. And as she runs, the Tall Ram waves farewell to her and then he looks across the street. There, he sees Mortimer with his case ducking into a public bathroom. Which is near Arty's Arcade.

The Tall Ram smiles and pulls out a small notebook.

"Nice..." he says.

****

Inside the public bathroom, Mortimer pushes open every dirty stall. All of them are empty, have brown water, and vile graffiti desecrates their green walls. With the coast clear, Mortimer locks the bathroom door and opens his case. He pulls out set of clothes, a large battery pack, a pair of gloves, and lots of wires, and he assembles his gear with haste.

****

Inside Arty's Arcade, Jayson sits on a vibrantly decorated half-wall with a large plate of food and a large drink. The plate is currently filthy with crumbs, sauces, and cheese, but it used to have a large serving of loaded nachos, two chili dogs, a microwaved bean burrito with a partially frozen middle, chicken wings, chicken tenders, and a small salad to balance it out. The drink is diet soda pop, and Jayson is sure they are out of syrup because all he tastes is carbonation, but he doesn't have enough money for a refill. So, he suffers the torture of pure carbonated liquid dissolving his insides.

While Jayson sips his awful drink, he watches kids play a fighting game. The flashing lights, chaotic noises of buttons clacking, explosions, gunshots, lasers, and low-quality screams mixing with loud music from the other games are hell on his ears, but he watches with great interest and has his weapon held close to his chest. As Jayson watches them, an older, fat rabbit with patchy brown and black fur and a thin, black tuft of hair approaches him and leans on the wall next to him. This is the owner, Owen Owenheim.

"Hey," says Owen.

"Hey," replies Jayson. "You really turned this place around."

"Yeah, it was a good investment. If things keep up like this, I'll have it paid off in three years."

Jayson nods, smiling thinly. "Good... good."

The two are silent for a few more seconds, watching the patrons play arcade games or control their children with various degrees of success. Then Owen breaks the silence with a sigh and a quick drum on the wall.

"So... I heard you and Lexia got into a fight again," says Owen.

"It happens," says Jayson.

"You do know Lexia is going to kill you one day?"

"That'll be the day."

"I'm not joking, Jayson. She's a freak. Stay away from her."

"I'm not scared of her."

"You should be."

"Fear is a weakness that is easily exploitable. So, I live fearlessly, even when dealing with Lexia. It is the way to go."

Owen scoffs and pulls away from the wall. "Yeah... Okay. I'm just going to do prize inventory... Weirdo."

Owen walks away and Jayson smiles to himself as his grip tightens around his weapon. But the serenity is ruined when a car screeches. His ears perk up, he whips around, and immediately dives off the half-wall, tackling a kid onto the ground.

An unseen force flings a car through the arcade entrance, spraying the lobby with shattered glass and splintered brick. People scream and scatter as Jayson scrambles to take cover behind another half-wall with the kid, who is trembling in his grip.

The car skids along the floor until it slams into the wall Jayson was sitting on just seconds ago, sputtering out smoke and its engine crackling. After a few seconds of heavy silence, Jayson releases the kid and shoos him away.

"Find your parents and run," says Jayson.

The kid runs away and Jayson peeks out from the corner. His ears droop and his eyes widen when the car is shoved to the side by an invisible force, destroying the prize booth and nearly hitting Owen. Seconds later, a shadow stretches across the floor, and Jayson narrows his eyes.

"What the hell?" says Jayson.

In the doorway is a red fox with the right side of his face scarred, his right ear mangled, and comb-over styled dark hair. His size puts him towering over the other rabbits, and a battery pack is strapped on his back, powering his mechanical gloves. He is also dressed in flashy garb decorated with bold, yellow lightning bolts on his sleeves and collar. Mortimer Walters has arrived.

"Come on out, Hobo. I know you're in here," says Mortimer.

Mortimer steps further in, passing rabbits cowering and shivering in fear.

"*Wheeeere aaaare youuuu?*" sings Mortimer. Then he suddenly stops, slowly turns to Jayson and grins. His gloves spark. Then they glow and hum, and a metal pole is ripped off the wall and flies into his hand while metallic debris rises to surround his other hand. "There you are."

****

At Samantha's Spa, Lexia is still sitting in the lobby, but now she has moved near a display of lotions, shampoos, and dyes, all of which are locked in small cases. Her foot rapidly taps the floor, her fingers drum on her hand, and she looks around anxiously while occasionally reading a label. As she alternates between reading labels and scanning the lobby, her spine tingles, and her fingers twitch as she looks around some more. While she scans the area, her eyes catch something outside. She didn't mean to look outside, but what she sees gives her pause. Then her eyes widen, and she throws the nearest rabbit to the floor.

"Everyone duck!" yells Lexia.

Suppressed gunfire rattles. Wood and glass shatter, and bottles of shampoo and care products explode, showering the area with fragrant goo and debris. The bullets destroyed the area Lexia was sitting at, and she flips the display table and crouches behind it while the customers scream and scatter. When the shooting stops, Lexia peeks around the table and growls.

Claribel Belle Blair enters the building with a drum magazine in her gun, and her eyes are focused on the upturned table as she takes careful steps towards Lexia, her tongue flicking out and tasting the air.

"Lexia Hartwick let's not make this harder than it has to be," says Claribel.

Claribel walks further in, and Lexia reaches for her knife sheathed on the back of her belt. Claribel's tongue flicks the air again as she continues her careful approach.

Then she shoots.

The bullets tear apart the table and wall, and Lexia leaps away, jumps and dodges bullets, and she throws the knife.

Claribel deflects the knife with her rifle, which gives Lexia enough time to close the distance and draw another knife.

She swipes at Claribel, and the snake blocks it and continues to do so as Lexia slashes at her. What's left of the crowd scatters, and Claribel whacks Lexia to the floor.

Lexia rolls to her feet and throws the knife when Claribel shoots again. The knife goes into Claribel's shoulder, causing her shots to go wild. The snake hisses in pain, and Lexia charges her and rams her into the customer service counter, which is still being occupied by Mariana, who calmly moves to the side in her rolling chair with a romance book in hand, still bored despite the chaos in the lobby.

Lexia attempts to punch Claribel, but her punch is deflected. Claribel slams Lexia on the counter and yanks out the knife in her shoulder. Then she lunges at Lexia and—

****

Jayson leaps and rolls while Mortimer launches jagged metal bits at him with swift flicks of his hand while his other hand holds his metal pole tight. The sharp projectiles are impaled in the walls and arcade games, and Jayson draws his weapon, becomes engulfed in a faint blue aura, and bats away a long, sharp piece of metal that slows down by a fraction when entering the aura space.

A few more pieces are launched, but Jayson deflects them, leaving the arcade wrecked with metal slabs sticking out of the floor, walls, ceiling, and games.

"I haven't seen you in these parts before," says Jayson after whacking away the last piece and disabling the aura.

"Yeah, no shit. I just got here," says Mortimer.

"So, who are you supposed to be?"

"I'm your dad sent from the future to the past to kill you in order to save the world!"

Jayson sneers. "That's the plot for Deathbot 4!"

Mortimer twirls his pole, his fangs gleaming as he grins. He and Jayson circle each other in the destroyed lobby, glass crunching under their feet and the air discolored from the haze of lingering dust.

"Ah, I see you're a Deathbot fan," says Mortimer.

"I just had the misfortune of watching it," says Jayson.

"Misfortune? It was a good movie."

"No, it wasn't. Deathbot 3 was the last good film in the franchise, and the rest have been garbage."

"What!" Mortimer points his pole at Jayson. "Deathbot 3 retconned everything about Deathbot 1 and 2! Deathbot 4 fixed what that movie ruined! You probably thought Deathbot: Reclamation was award-worthy with that kind of stupid opinion."

Jayson aims his wooden weapon at Mortimer. "You called Deathbot 4 'good.' Your opinions are null and void regarding the Deathbot franchise."

Mortimer narrows his eyes, as does Jayson. Their muscles tense under their clothes, and both tighten their grips on their weapons.

"By the way, Mama Bear sent me to kill you," says Mortimer.

"She better get a refund, then," says Jayson.

Mortimer growls, and he extends his hand to the rubble. His glove glows, and forks, butter knives, and spoons rise in the air, creating a ball of metal. Jayson's eye twitches and Mortimer grins. Then he launches them at Jayson, and the Hobo Warrior activates the aura.

****

Back at Samantha's Spa, Lexia crashes through a door and rolls across the floor of a massage room. Claribel stomps after her, hissing and tail rattling. Lexia gets up and wipes blood from her face and grins.

"Okay... I'll admit, you're a tough one," says Lexia.

She stumbles back to regain her footing while Claribel keeps approaching, eyes narrowed and tail still rattling with her rifle slung on her back.

"But if you think I'm afraid of wrecking your pretty scales, I got news for you," says Lexia.

Claribel punches Lexia in the nose, and then grabs her arm and swings her onto the floor. Lexia groans irritably and Claribel draws her pistol.

"Mama Bear gives her regards," says Claribel.

She aims, and Lexia suddenly twists Claribel's hand. The pistol goes off, grazing Lexia, and Claribel yelps and is quickly beaten down with heavy strikes from Lexia's fists.

Claribel tries to get up, but Lexia kicks her to the floor. When Lexia goes for a stomp, Claribel's tail grabs her leg and tugs her down.

Lexia falls flat on her back, knocking the wind out of her. Then Claribel quickly gets up and uses her tail to throw Lexia into the wall.

The wall cracks on impact, and Lexia falls to the floor. Claribel grabs her pistol, and right as she aims at Lexia, the harlequin-hare rushes her and slams into her. A gunshot goes off, leaving Lexia's ears ringing, and they both fall to the floor with a loud thud.

Claribel attempts to aim her pistol at Lexia's head, but Lexia slams the pistol down, causing another shot to go off. Lexia follows up with a swift punch to Claribel's snout.

Claribel yelps and quickly knees Lexia off. And while the hybrid regains her footing, Claribel slithers around, wraps her limps around Lexia, and forces her to the floor again.

The two yell and curse as they roll around, knocking over another table. During the struggle, Claribel grabs Lexia's hair and starts smashing her face repeatedly into the floor.

****

At Arty's Arcade, Jayson uses his shoulder to push open a door and he stumbles inside with forks all over his bloody, scratched, and bruised body. He closes the door with his foot and winces as he pulls down a rack to block the door.

Jayson stumbles away and removes the forks, growling painfully as each utensil leaves small bloody holes on his body. The door rumbles and rattles. Jayson looks behind him and recoils when the door and rack are blasted into the wall across the room. Broken brick and thick dust rolls through the air, and Mortimer strolls through the gaping hole.

"Jayson! Stop running! You're just wasting our time that way!" says Mortimer.

Jayson's eyes narrow and everything darkens as he goes to tunnel vision. In the dark world surrounding Jayson, a white-eyed figure watches him, slithering through the void. Its smile spreads as Jayson charges, leaps, and punches Mortimer in the ear.

Mortimer stumbles, holding his ear and cursing up a storm. Jayson deals swift, hard blows to Mortimer and finishes with a kick that sends him rolling down the hall.

Jayson draws his cosmic-wood sword after that, and approaches Mortimer while the the specter watches him, eager to see what is to come.

****

At the spa, Claribel has her tail wrapped around Lexia's throat and is pinning her against the wall. Lexia grunts and gags for air; her lungs burn, and her eyes roll back as she tries to pry the tail off, but it is no use.

"I'll give you credit where credit is due. You made this exhilarating," says Claribel.

Lexia lifts enough of Claribel's tail to sink her teeth into it, and Claribel shrieks painfully and throws Lexia through the wall across the room.

Lexia rolls across the floor as a bloodied mess, but quickly leaps back up. She staggers a bit before she gets her footing, and she giggles madly as she wipes her mouth.

Okay, she's definitely a tough cookie. I need to end this before she gets desperate, thinks Lexia.

Claribel climbs through the hole, and Lexia flips her off and runs down the hallway. Claribel gives chase while un-slinging her rifle, and Lexia looks over her shoulder and dives around a corner when Claribel shoots at her.

Lexia ducks into a storage room and seeks cover behind a rack stocked with scented oils and other spa products. A few seconds later, Claribel opens the door and cautiously enters with her rifle raised.

Claribel's tongue flicks the air as she searches the area for any sign of Lexia.

Meanwhile, Lexia silently creeps around the racks while unscrewing a bottle of scented oil. When Claribel's back is to her, she hurls the bottle and it smashes open against the snake's back, staining her coat, hair, and hat in pink oil.

Claribel hisses and shoots blindly at Lexia, destroying everything around her, filling the air with the intense scents of gunpowder, lotions, and oils.

As the bullets fly, Lexia stays low and grabs the nearest shampoo bottle, unscrews it, and throws it as hard as she can at Claribel, hitting her shoulder.

Claribel staggers from the impact, and Lexia charges and tackles her. The pair tumble violently, rolling over each other across the slick floor until they come to a stop with Lexia on top. Claribel instantly kicks Lexia off and lunges at her, screaming madly, before the hybrid can recover.

Upon impact, they grapple and wrestle on the floor, both cursing and screaming as they get covered in cleaning products. Punches and kicks fly, and hair is tugged between them until Lexia finally manages to get behind Claribel and put her in a choke hold.

She squeezes tight, slowly cutting off Claribel's breath until the snake's thrashing fades away.

Lexia's heart pounds as she waits a few more seconds before letting go of Claribel and scrambling back. Using the racks for support, she manages to stand up and starts staggering towards the door.

However, her ears catch the sound of trash shifting behind her. She quickly turns around and sees Claribel with an icy glare, reaching for her rifle.

Lexia's eyes dart around until they fall on a fire extinguisher nearby. She lunges for it as bullets whiz past her, and then Lexia swings the extinguisher at Claribel with a vicious yell.

The impact of metal against bone thunders through the room and Claribel flies off her feet. The snake slides across the floor and comes to a stop upon hitting a rack, and Lexia sprints out the door, leaving Claribel limp on the ground.

****

The world is still dim around Jayson in the hallway of Arty's Arcade, and the dark figure with white eyes still watches him, clinging to the ceiling with thin red lines on their wrists.

Jayson and Mortimer are engaged in furious close-quarters combat, both using their skills in an attempt to gain an edge over the other. Jayson wields his cosmic weapon with precision to parry, block, and fend off Mortimer's violent strikes with his metal pole.

With each deflection of Jayson's weapon, Mortimer unleashes another relentless onslaught of fast swipes that Jayson has difficulty dealing with, despite the aura manipulation. But with both fighters stuck in a perpetual stalemate, Mortimer extends his electromagnetic glove towards a nearby metal door.

The glove hums, his battery pack glows, and sparks of power surround it as the door is ripped from its moorings, taking part of the wall with it. He yells out a war cry and slams the door into Jayson, sending him hurtling into the wall with a thunderous crash.

The door falls to the ground with Jayson, leaving behind an imprint of the bunny's body embedded in the plaster. Mortimer then approaches Jayson and slowly unsheathes claws, staring down at him with pure annoyance pulsating in his eyes.

"It's been fun, but I need to kill you, so... Yeah," says Mortimer.

Jayson pushes himself up and wipes blood off his face.

"It's nothing personal, Hobo. But a guy's gotta eat," continues Mortimer.

Mortimer lunges, and Jayson grabs Mortimer and uses the momentum to slam him into the wall, and then he yells and throws Mortimer into the room that the door was yanked from. The room contains soda syrup and CO_2 canisters that lay neatly stacked.

Mortimer pushes himself up from the floor, just to get a flying kick to the chest by Jayson. He hits the wall of soda syrup and the safety valves break, spraying him and his equipment with a sticky mess. The only one that didn't spray out anything was the diet soda pop container.

Mortimer's gloves and battery pack spark, smoke, and dim, and Mortimer inspects himself, grimacing at his filthy situation.

"Huh... This is an interesting way to go. Kudos to you, bro," says Mortimer, offering Jayson a small smile.

Jayson runs up with his wooden sword, yells, and whacks Mortimer's head. The fox crumbles, and Jayson whacks him a few more times. When he is done, he is panting heavily, and speckles of blood are on his weapon.

Then Jayson stumbles back. The world brightens, showing the carnage of the fight. The specter disappears, and Jayson looks around while wiping his sword against his sleeve. After that, he sheaths his weapons and runs out of the room, leaving Mortimer to soak in blood and soda.

When Fixers Come to Town

Outside in a random alley, Jayson skids to a stop and seeks cover behind a dumpster, panting and wiping blood and sweat from his face. With the coast clear, he sits down and stares at the brick wall in front of him. It has a winged DNA strand painted above wall art of a grim reaper using their scythe to spread a toxic cloud over a city of people dissolving into skeletons. And the picture also has graffiti over it, saying *"Come See with Me"* and *"Reel Sight Is Better Than Real Sight"* with blue dots and colorful butterflies surrounding the words and a cartoony head of a female bear offering eyeballs.

Jayson stares at the odd pictures, struggling to catch his breath and cope with the throbbing pain all over his body. Several seconds later, Lexia runs around a corner, tripping and falling over a rusted tricycle.

"Crap!" curses Lexia.

Jayson watches Lexia, and when she sees Jayson, she jumps up and brushes herself off, playing it cool as she approaches him, even though she is a bloody and bruised mess soaked in body cleaning products.

"Wassup?" says Lexia.

"Rough day?" asks Jayson.

"Nope. You?"

"Same."

Lexia sits next to Jayson, and they stare at the wall in front of them; both quiet while the world moves around them with sirens in the distance.

"So... Lexia..." begins Jayson.

"Yes, Jayson?" says Lexia stiffly.

"Any weirdos, today?"

"Some snake with a mobster fetish. You?"

"A snake?" says Jayson curiously.

Lexia nods. "Yeah. Snake. Had one of those uh..." She wags her hand. "Rattle thingies on her tail."

"Oh wow... I hadn't seen one in a while."

"Dealing with her was super easy, though. Hardly any inconvenience. How about you?"

Jayson winces and stretches his legs. "I got attacked by an ugly fox with some kind of weird electro-magnetic equipment. He was easy too. Just a quick bop on the head and he was done."

"We're way too good at this."

"Yep."

"Yep..."

"Yep..."

The two sit in silence for a few more seconds. Then Derrick lands nearby and approaches them while lighting a cigarette. As he walks towards them, Jayson and Lexia use each other for support to stand up. Once they are close enough to Derrick, Lexia punches him in the shoulder; he is unfazed by this.

"There you are!" says Lexia. "Where were you when I was dealing with a snake?"

"Or a crazy fox with an electro-magnetic device?" adds Jayson.

"I was on the shitter because of Taco King," says Derrick.

Lexia points at Jayson. "Ha! I told you Taco King sucks!"

Jayson rolls his eyes, and Derrick puffs out some smoke.

"But there is good news. We've got Mama Bear nervous; that is why she sent a pair of Fixers," says Derrick. "But seeing as how you two handled them quite well, I don't think they'll be a problem. So, how about we get you two cleaned up and then we grab a bite to eat? I got coupons that are about to expire, and I need some more protein after my explosive weight loss."

Lexia once again smirks at Jayson, and he looks between her and Derrick.

"Oh, come on. You two just have weak stomachs," says Jayson.

"You have the stomach from Hell, Jayson. We can't compete with you," says Derrick. "Now, how about some lunch? I'm buying."

Jayson and Lexia look at each other, Jayson motions Lexia ahead, and the pair gingerly follows Derrick out of the alley. As they leave, they don't see the Tall Ram leaning against a lamp post, writing notes.

****

At the safehouse, Rolland, Dacre, Cyrus, and Shae are playing One-O around the coffee table when the door opens, spilling the afternoon sunlight on them with a pair of shadows stretching across the floor. The group looks at the doorway and sees Claribel and Mortimer standing there, bloodied, bruised, and soaked in soda syrup and beauty care products. Both of them are wearing bandages from a supermarket medical kit and are stiff, with Claribel wearing an icepack taped to her head.

Rolland's group silently stares at them, and Mortimer steps aside and motions Claribel inside. She walks in, followed by Mortimer, who closes and locks the door. Neither of them says anything as they walk past Rolland's group to get to the stairs.

"Bad day, eh?" says Rolland.

"Bug off," grunts Claribel.

"What she said," says Mortimer.

The pair continue up the stairs and quietly go to their respective rooms to change.

For Claribel, once she is in her room, she goes to her suitcase, removes a fresh set of clothes in an air-sealed bag and a cleaning kit for scales, high quality shampoo, and a fluffy towel and a green bathrobe with brown and gold letters spelling "*Block World*" stitched on the back. She also sets a plastic sheet on her floor, followed by a felt sheet, and sets her weapons on the floor, along with a gun-cleaning kit.

For Mortimer, his room is a mess and has a small fridge in the closet. He winces as he removes his equipment, and he discards his clothes, revealing burn and shrapnel scars covering the right side of his neck and extending down to his shoulder and upper chest. He tosses his sticky clothes aside, and carefully puts his equipment in his armored case. Then he opens up a worn-out suitcase and pulls out a plastic grocery bag holding a set of clothes stuffed inside, plus a towel and a grooming kit.

Claribel and Mortimer exit their rooms, with Claribel wearing her bathrobe and Mortimer wearing plaid pajamas. They nod politely to each other and go into separate bathrooms. Shortly after, the showers start. Steam pours out from under the doors, and Rolland's group stares at the ceiling, listening to the sounds of rushing water for a few more seconds before Rolland tosses a card on the table.

"By the way. One-O," says Rolland.

Dacre drops his card on Rolland's card. "Wild. Red."

Cyrus grins and plops a red "6" on the stack.

"One-O," says Cyrus.

Shae drops a blue "6" on top of the red card.

"One-O with a blue-o, loser," says Shae.

****

Not The Crystal Plate is a perfectly mediocre restaurant. It is modest in appearance, with neutral colors that keep everything relaxed. Its prices are fair, the orders come out fast, and its food is worth neither a glowing review nor harsh condemnation. It is affordable for the poor and middle class alike, even with the poison of inflation killing their hard-earned money.

It is because it is in a perfectly middle ground state that Derrick has decided to take Lexia and Jayson there. They had to use the restaurant bathroom to clean themselves off of grime and blood before sitting down, and even though they did clean off their bodies, their clothes are still stained with the aftermath of their fights.

That said, they are still welcomed in, and Jayson finds the atmosphere welcoming as clanking dishes and the murmuring of people float through the air. And even though it is simple, Jayson's favorite part of the restaurant is not the food, but the logo painted big enough for everyone to see with "*NOT THE CRYSTAL PLATE*" on it and a wooden plate beneath the words.

Derrick sits across from Lexia and Jayson in their corner of the restaurant, and all are looking at their menus and having drinks of mostly shaved ice.

Jayson and Derrick are looking at their menus normally, but Lexia has turned her menu into a wall between her and Jayson and is using the dessert menu to block herself from Derrick.

At the far end of the restaurant, watching Jayson's group, is the Tall Ram. He is stirring a protein mix into a large cup of water and has an almond-crusted chicken, scrambled eggs with lintels, a side of cottage cheese, and a peanut butter milkshake. His coat is slung over his chair and his golfer's cap is on the table, so the world sees his thick hair dyed in metallic silver, turquoise, and cherry red. His odd appearance and meals have brought some eyes to him, but he ignores them, choosing to keep his focus on Jayson, Lexia, and Derrick.

While watching the people of interest, Mariana Cross approaches Derrick's table, pen and pad in hand, and her dim blue eyes still heavy from her misery.

"Are you ready to order yet?" asks Mariana.

"Yes, I would like the salmon supreme meal please," says Derrick.

"Kids mac n' cheese, please," says Jayson.

"Get something bigger. I'm buying, remember?" says Derrick.

"Fine. Adult mac 'n cheese, please."

"And I would love your fettuccine broccoli alfredo. Extra garlic and onions," says Lexia.

Jayson sneers at Lexia, but he can't see her smirking behind the menu wall.

Mariana writes the orders, yanks away the menus, and leaves without a word.

Meanwhile, the Tall Ram keeps watching the group from his table, his pen tapping his notebook slowly while his other hand continues stirring his protein mix. Then a little device buzzes in his pocket. He pulls out a flip phone and flicks it open to answer it, getting odd and bewildered looks from a nearby table.

"Trafford Augustine speaking," says the Tall Ram.

"Status update," says a stilted voice on the other end.

Trafford smiles. "Mr. Exe, I was just thinking about you."

"Status update."

"Bliss Town appears to have our missing guy. And there is an interesting variable that we did not anticipate."

"*Explain.*"

"The Reel Sight distributed from this area has the qualities of our missing subject. But the unforeseen variable is Jayson Hopper, the Hobo Warrior Bunny, as they call him. He has an object that warps time around him by one second. It's very peculiar and will require more data."

"*What about Lexia Hartwick and Derrick Marlow?*"

"Nothing noticeable with them yet. Lexia is still nuts and Derrick is just a grouch. I will need more time to properly analyze them."

"*Keep me updated. Enjoy your milkshake.*"

"You too."

Trafford cringes immediately after, and Mr. Exe's end clicks off. Trafford then puts the phone away and watches Derrick's group intently. His assignment at Bliss Town is definitely going to be interesting.

II

A Bad Day

Mortimer Walters spends the day trying to kill the Hobo Warrior Bunny. And all Jayson Hopper wants to do is relax.

A Bad Day- 01

The cracks in the sky warp the sun and any clouds that go near them, and yet the afternoon light shines brightly on the dying buildings of Bliss Town. Even though the town is hell, there is still life in the decay. The chirping songbirds rest in the trees and on the powerlines, children play in crumbling parks and dead grass, and cars are bumper to bumper outside of the best fast-food joint in town. Taco King.

The rugged sign has yet to be updated or repaired, so the same smiling taco with a crown has faded colors and a cracked shell, partially exposing its large light-tubes. The taco waves at the citizens of Bliss Town with its ball-shaped hand, and cars bully each other to get into the drive-thru or parking lot. No amount of sunshine or chirping birds will calm them down until they get those delicious tacos.

The rundown building that is Taco King is currently being repainted, bringing out bright yellow and red colors. Next to the door is a sign that says: ***"TACO TUESDAY SALE! 4 TACOS FOR 16 BUCKS!"***

The cars honk, angry people shout, and the clog in the street gradually worsens as more customers line up to get in on the amazing deal. But while they are distracted, Jayson rolls out of a nearby bush, his hand tightly clutching his wooden sword's hilt. His eyes snap around, his nose and ears twitch, and then his eyes lock on a dumpster guarded by one wall of fencing. Jayson grins with a needy glint in his eyes, runs, and leaps on the fence. Then he climbs the old, splintered post and dives into the dumpster.

A minute later, Jayson jumps out, covered in bits of food, sauce, and other nasty things. In his hands is a bag filled with half-eaten burritos and soggy tacos and nachos. But right as he leaves the dumpster, an old squirrel, wearing the Taco King uniform, greasy from hard work, rushes towards Jayson with a broom. This is Juarez Gomez.

"Hey, dick nugget! What are you doing in my trash!" yells Juarez.

"I'm getting lunch," replies Jayson calmly.

"Go dig in the Crystal Plate's trash! Leave my trash alone!"

"Lexia won't let me on her side."

"I don't care. Get lost before I sodomize you with this broom!"

Jayson holds up his hand and bows his head in mock submission. "Alright, alright, relax. I'm outta here."

Juarez walks away, shaking his head, and Jayson huffs and looks at his food.

"I'm going to need some hot sauce with this," says Jayson.

****

Meanwhile, inside the Taco King, the entrance bell dings and Mortimer walks in, wearing his raccoon mask and dressed in a simple blue suit with a white dress shirt. The mask and suit do an excellent job covering his old scars and new bruises, but not even the mask can hide his annoyance when he sees how full the lobby is. And a plague of disgust surges through him when he sees a large group of fat rabbits waddle away from the counter and go to the soda machine. The rest of the lobby is filled with customers of equal or greater fat, and Mortimer shudders and forces himself to go forward.

"It's like a pod of whales," grumbles Mortimer.

When he reaches the counter, he smiles at a pretty white-furred, female lop-eared rabbit with brown ears and dark curly hair. Her tag says "Mariana," and she looks like she'd rather be anywhere else besides stuck behind a cash register at a fast-food joint.

"What do you want?" says Mariana Cross.

Mortimer leans against the counter and smiles pleasantly. "Hello there, darling. I'd like the number five, King Don Burrito meal."

"Anything else?"

"A pleasant attitude from you will be nice."

"Not on the menu. That'll be twenty bucks."

Mortimer shakes his head and reaches into his wallet to pull out a wad of bills.

"I'll give you an extra twenty if you smile," says Mortimer.

"Tips are prohibited, as stated in chapter one subsection one of the King Food Enterprise Corporation Company Incorporated wagie manual. Also, bribing me will lead you down a dark path that ends with your suicide," says Mariana.

Mortimer sneers, and Mariana reaches under the counter and plops down a cup with a smiling taco on it.

"Your cup. Unless you want to upsize it to a large for an extra three fifty," says Mariana.

"Will I kill myself if I do?" asks Mortimer.

"No. But you'll get diabetes and lose your feet."

"Oh yeah? Which flavor soda?"

"All of them."

"The water?"

"We don't serve water here."

Mortimer snatches the cup and puts a twenty on the counter. "Keep the change. Unless I die from it or lose my feet."

"No, you're safe with that."

Mortimer grunts. "Good. Smile more. Maybe you'll make happier predictions."

"I won't," says Mariana.

She puts the money in the drawer and gives Mortimer his receipt, which has '318' printed on it, and Mortimer goes to the soda machine.

"Freakin' emos," grumbles Mortimer.

As this happens, Juarez returns to the front, Mariana gives the ticket to the backline workers, and Jayson enters the lobby. Passing Mortimer as he fills his cup, Jayson goes to the counter, tightly clutching his bag of trash food.

"Excuse me, can I get some hot sauce for my trash burrito?" asks Jayson.

Juarez sneers and points at Jayson. "Hey, I told you to get lost!"

"All I want is some sauce for the food you threw away," says Jayson.

"You think I'm playing when I said I was going to sodomize you with a broom?"

"I don't want to fight you, but if you put that broom anywhere near me, I will kick your balls straight through your mouth! Now give me some hot sauce so I can get out of here!"

"Screw that. I'd rather stick a broom up your ass."

"What the hell is up with you, brooms, and asses?"

"What the hell is up with you digging in my trash!"

"I'm a hobo!"

"Then get a job!"

Mortimer tops off his drink, snaps on the lid, and turns around to look at Juarez. "For the love of God, just give the guy some hot sauce. It's bad enough he has to eat out of the... trash."

Mortimer's voice drifts to silence and he and Jayson look at each other. Like gears closing a door, the more Jayson stares, the narrower his eyes become. The lobby gets quiet, the environment darkens, until all Jayson sees is Mortimer. The hobo's hand tightens around his weapon and Mortimer clamps his pistol's grip.

Time ticks by. The two continue staring at each other. Jayson's eyes and nose twitch, and Mortimer's claws extend as his eyes snap to Jayson's hand and face. Their ears twitch as the noise of lighthearted chatter, laughter, and an excited talking kid fade away.

The two enemies keep staring, hearts thumping, hands tensing, and eyes narrowing with their breaths going into forced regulations.

Suddenly the environment snaps back to life and Jayson releases his grip on his weapon the same time Mortimer slides his hand off his holster.

"Your voice sounds familiar," says Jayson.

"You look familiar," says Mortimer.

"Have we met?"

"I don't know. Have we?"

"Where's your weird equipment?"

"You mean the one you gunked up with soda syrup? Yeah, it needs new everything, so thanks for that, dipshit."

"You literally tried to kill me with a car. And cutlery. And a door."

Mariana returns with a tray of food and stares at the standoff, completely bored by what she sees. Juarez, meanwhile, has his hand on the phone.

"Order three-one-eight," says Mariana.

"That's my order," says Mortimer.

"Can you get some sauce for me?" asks Jayson.

"What kind of sauce?"

"Hot sauce."

"The kind that makes your throat bleed?"

"No. The kind that has a hard kick but is still forgiving."

"Do you want Kind of Mild Sauce, **Hobo?**" asks Mortimer.

"Yeah, I would, **Foxy,**" says Jayson.

"How many does the hobo want?" Mariana asks Mortimer.

"Well, Hobo?" asks Mortimer to Jayson, his eyes focused on Jayson's hand again.

"Five packets," replies Jayson.

Mortimer walks towards the counter, his steps slow and heavy, and Jayson moves away, keeping his eyes on Mortimer. Once at the counter, Mortimer slowly pulls out his wallet.

"Give the Hobo Warrior Bunny a large drink to wash down the trash, and I'll need five packets of your Sort Of Hot Sauce," says Mortimer.

"That'll be three-fifty," says Mariana.

Mortimer gives Mariana the money, and she gives him the change, cup, and sauce packets. Mortimer puts the packets in the cup and approaches Jayson. Once they are toe to toe, Jayson has to tilt his head up so he can meet Mortimer's eyes. The fox's whiskers shift from his muzzle twitching, and he holds the cup out to Jayson.

"How about we enjoy our meals, and when we're done, we can go back to killing each other," says Mortimer.

"Fine by me," says Jayson, taking the cup.

"Good."

Jayson shakes the packets into his bag of trash food, goes to the soda machine, and fills his cup with *Hi-B Tangerine Magma Burst*. Then he and Mortimer take their seats at opposite sides of the lobby, but within easy sight of each other.

The pair stare at each other in complete silence as they eat their meals, and after Jayson finishes eating, he goes to the bathroom, feeling Mortimer's eyes following him.

Once inside the bathroom, Jayson walks to the sink, sets his cup down, and tightly grips the off-white porcelain. His heart races, his breathing is heavy. His tired, baggy eyes stare back at him through the scratched mirror. The world dims, and behind Jayson is the Specter.

He stares at it through the mirror, and it looks back at him with its white void eyes. The black mass that is its head splits open, exposing a white abyss for the mouth. Before it can say anything, the bathroom door opens, and Mortimer walks through the Specter, causing it to disappear.

Jayson's heart races and his hands grip the sink tighter as he and Mortimer lock eyes through the reflection.

"You should have taken your time eating. Or tried running," says Mortimer.

"I didn't feel like doing either of those," says Jayson.

Mortimer locks the bathroom door and draws his pistol, and Jayson studies the fox through the mirror.

"Eh. Still should have tried," says Mortimer.

"Well, you're here, so go for it," says Jayson.

Mortimer aims his pistol and—

****

Out in the lobby, the cheerful chatter of the customers and annoyed shouts of the workers are interrupted by gunshots and shattering glass coming from the bathroom. People scream and dive down or run out the back door.

More sporadic gunshots and breaking porcelain echo from the bathroom, and Mariana calmly drinks from a small cup while Juarez and the other employees duck for cover.

A few seconds later, Mortimer flies through the bathroom door and hits the wall, knocking a framed advertisement loose. But he quickly gets back up and rushes inside the bathroom.

The bathroom is a wreck of destroyed mirrors, and broken stalls and toilets. Bullet holes cover the walls and shattered tiles and glass litter the floor as water pumps from the damaged sinks and toilets. Mortimer's pistol is in the corner, and Jayson and Mortimer exchange brutal punches and kicks; they block and deflect what they can, bouncing off the walls, breaking more tiles and crashing through more stalls.

They roll around each other, their claws tearing at each other's skin and clothes, and when Mortimer attempts to bite Jayson, he slams his hand under the fox's chin, forcing it shut.

Then Jayson kicks Mortimer off, but before he can fully recover, Mortimer scrambles to his feet, grabs Jayson, and slams his head into the wall.

Jayson's ears ring and his vision spins as blood trickles down his head. Mortimer grabs a broken piece of toilet and goes for a stab.

Jayson swiftly grabs Mortimer's wrist and uses his momentum to swing him into another stall, breaking it to pieces. The two stumble around, feet splashing in the filthy toilet water.

Jayson kicks out Mortimer's footing, headbutts him, and flips him onto the floor. Then he stomps on Mortimer's head, making the fox limp, and Jayson stumbles back, breathing heavily and clutching his racing heart.

When Mortimer remains motionless, Jayson grabs his cup off the floor, shakes out the toilet water, and goes to the lobby. He ignores the horrified stares of the remaining guests as he refills his drink.

After that, he grabs a handful of napkins and presses them against the gash on his head but stops abruptly when he feels an odd sensation running through his spine. He turns around and sees Mariana staring at him, still bored.

They look at each other for a few more seconds before Jayson shakes his head and exits Taco King.

Outside, the sun is warm, and the parking lot and drive-thru are empty, making Jayson's walk easy. He sips his drink and presses the napkins harder against his head as blood seeps down his cheek and stains his hand and wrist. Sirens wail in the distance, but he doesn't care. Today is just another day for the Hobo Warrior Bunny.

A Bad Day- 02

Jayson's steps are quick and directionless as he walks the streets of Bliss Town. His head wound has hardened to a sticky scab, and a thin layer of blood has stained his white fur, brown hair, and blue scarf. But that is not bothering him in the slightest. Partly because he is used to the violence, and partly because the *Hi-B Tangerine Magma Burst* is proving to be a great, sweet, and tangy flavored opiate.

While Jayson walks down the street, sipping his drink, he passes Arty's Arcade, which has police tape and plywood covering its gaping hole. He keeps walking in a trance-like state, sucking up the tangerine soda, and passing murals of rabbit soldiers in gas masks fighting in trenches, and a globe surrounded by a green mist. As he passes the mural, police cars pass him, and moments later, the cup runs dry. He throws the cup in a trash can and sits on a bench.

Jayson takes a deep breath, closes his eyes, and slouches in his seat as he slowly exhales. But the moment of peace ends as quickly as it begins. His ears twitch to the sound of a rapidly approaching whistle. His eyes snap open and he barely registers what he is seeing while his legs launch him away from the bench.

A rocket detonates directly on the bench. Jayson and pieces of the blasted wooden seat hurtle into the morning sky. Jayson crashes onto the sidewalk but springs back up almost immediately, hand firmly clasped around his weapon's hilt and his body throbbing from pain and anger.

Another rocket is fired at him, but he bats it away with a powerful swing. The projectile careens wildly and slams into a nearby tree. The force of the blast blows out a chunk of the tree, causing it to collapse on itself in an impressive display of splinters.

He snaps his attention to the source of the missile on a roof several buildings down, and he narrows his eyes as the world darkens around him. With a throaty growl, he takes off in a sprint down the sidewalk until he finally reaches the building.

Jayson jumps up and grabs the closest windowsill. Then he rapidly scurries up multiple levels, using his legs and core to propel him up each level while his fingers grip everything tightly. As soon as he clears the roof's edge, he sees Lexia waiting with her bazooka pointed at him.

Jayson yells, rushes Lexia, and whacks her with his cosmic-wood sword hard enough to create a shock wave inside the aura that cracks the roof and shatters glass.

The destructive force of the energy tears Lexia's body into pieces, with her head and arm flying away like debris floating in molasses, her bazooka shattering, and her torso breaking apart.

Jayson pants heavily, and the darkness leaves his sight, and the aura vanishes, allowing everything to crumble as it should. As soon as that happens, he realizes that there is straw stuffing all over the roof; and there is a smiley face drawn on the scarecrow head mimicking Lexia's features. This brings Jayson's brain to fizzle and pop.

"What the heck?" says Jayson.

A gun cocks, Jayson whirls around and diverts the pistol right as Lexia (wearing fluffy pink earmuffs) pulls the trigger. The bullet whizzes into the sky and Jayson punches Lexia in the face, knocking her earmuffs off.

Lexia stumbles back, holding her nose with blood seeping past her fingers. Her voice is warped to a squeaky tone as she curses and stomps in circles, but Jayson frowns at her, not in the least bit sorry.

"Ow! What the heck, Jayson!" cries Lexia.

"What do you mean what the heck? I should be the one saying what the heck to you! You tried killing me again!" says Jayson.

Lexia, still clutching her nose, draws her knife and swings it at Jayson. He blocks it and uses fancy footwork and precise motions to evade and block her other swipes.

"You're on my side! I was defending my territory!" says Lexia.

Jayson blocks a few more swipes from Lexia, both of them moving in a circle as wood and steel clash on the roof.

"I'm not on your side!" says Jayson.

Then Jayson disarms Lexia, trips her, and pins her down on the cracked roof, his body on top of hers, nose to nose. Both are growling.

"**You** are on my side. That bench was on my side!" says Jayson.

"No, it's not! It's next to Arty's Arcade! Which is on my side!" says Lexia.

Jayson thinks for a moment, reluctantly releases Lexia, and goes to the edge of the roof. It is an awkward angle, but he sees the crater where the bench used to be, and near it is Arty's Arcade. Which is when it registers that he is, in fact, on Lexia's side.

"Crap. She's right... Man, Derrick really sucks at making maps," says Jayson.

"Hey, Jayson!" calls Lexia.

Jayson groans. "What?"

He turns around and next thing he knows, he is blinded by a bright light, a wave of heat washes over him, and a strong force launches him and pieces of masonry into the sky. Everything is a messy blend of colors as Jayson screams and sails through the air with a trail of smoke.

Jayson's limbs flail as he twirls through the air, and when he starts falling, a truck labeled as "Paulie's Pillows" drives by, and Jayson lands through its trailer, shaking the truck. But the truck keeps going, and inside the trailer is Jayson, who is face first, sprawled out on many pillows with a Jayson-shaped hole in the roof. He is black and smoking and bits of blood are staining the pillows.

"I hate her," groans Jayson.

****

Meanwhile, far away from the commotion, at the edge of Bliss Town, Mortimer Walters stomps his way down the driveway to the safehouse, gripping his beloved raccoon mask tightly in his hands. He passes thorny weeds, dead bushes, a lawnmower that has somehow been consumed by a tree, and an ominous mailbox wrapped in razor wire. The cheerful chirping birds and dazzling sunlight seem to be mocking Mortimer's sour mood and the foul toilet water stench he is carrying with him.

Mortimer unlocks the door to the safehouse and steps into a whole new world. A clean world. A world where the carpet has been returned to its gray colors after a deep cleaning, the stains on the walls have been removed, the couch shows its true burgundy colors, and the furniture is dusted.

Mortimer stops in the doorway, staring with wide eyes at the wonderful sight. Even the air smells like pine cones. He hears dishes clanking in the kitchen, and he looks at the floor again. It is still damp from the steam cleaning, and his shoes are filthy from mud and other things, so he carefully takes off his shoes and puts them on a rack. Then he walks to the kitchen, where Claribel is.

The kitchen is spotless, and Claribel is scrubbing a large pan. She is wearing an apron and large cleaning gloves, as well as pajamas with colorful blocks on them, and a pistol is holstered on a belt around her waist.

Claribel grumbles to herself, taking all her frustration out on the pan with her scrub pad. The sink and adjacent counter are full of dirty dishes, but there is a rack of clean dishes sparkling in the sunlight. As Claribel cleans, her tongue flicks out, and she pauses while Mortimer goes to the freezer.

Claribel turns around, and Mortimer pulls out a pint of moose track ice cream. Her eyes widen at Mortimer's battered state, and she drops the pan in the black, bubbly water.

"Oh my God! What happened?" says Claribel.

Mortimer presses the pint against his head. "I had a run-in with the Hobo Warrior Bunny. Dude's a dick. All I want to do is kill him, and he goes ape shit. I've never dealt with a maniac like him before."

Claribel huffs and pulls off her gloves. "First your gear, now this. We should ask Mama Bear for more money. And now that I think about it, the Bazooka Bunny is kind of crazy, too. Our pay needs to be doubled."

"We can't ask her for more money until the job is done. So, I'm going to take a shower, and then look for the Hobo again."

Mortimer tries to leave the kitchen, but Claribel quickly grabs his arm.

"Wait, you need to rest for a while," says Claribel.

Mortimer gently pries Claribel off his arm. "No. I have a job to do."

"You're being stubborn, you know that, right?" says Claribel.

"Well, sorry for not taking Mama Bear's job lightly. I kinda don't want to be put in a barrel of acid. Unless you want to swap places with me, so you look while I relax," says Mortimer.

"Can't. My contract clearly states I get Mondays, Wednesdays, and Fridays off. And I use those days for personal time. Well, except for today. I spent all day cleaning this place. But it was filthy, so it had to be clean."

"You have a contract?"

"Yeah... Why? You don't?"

"No! Man, that's not fair! Mama Bear didn't even mention contracts when I joined her team."

Suddenly, red lights start swirling in the living room, and techno music plays through hidden speakers. Mortimer and Claribel draw their pistols and hurry to the living room. Upon entering, they find themselves stuck in a twilight zone of tension and confusion as the carpeted floor splits open and an elevator rises with colorful smoke pouring out. As the elevator rises, so do Mortimer and Claribel's gazes until their heads are tilted up to meet the eyes of the newcomer.

Towering over the pair is a smiling, muscular ram with black fur, gray spots, and a white mane with blood-red eyes. He has green rings on his wrists and neck and is wearing a lab coat over an armor-padded blue suit. The gift baskets contain fruits, candies, meat snacks, body and hair care products for foxes and snakes, and gift cards. One has a snake head and the other has a fox head taped to the baskets.

When the elevator locks in place, both sides stare at each other in silence, with the colorful smoke rolling and thinning out as it travels along the floor.

Several more seconds of silence pass, with Mortimer's eyes briefly flicking to Claribel before locking on the ram. Claribel's eyes also dart to Mortimer for a brief second before focusing on the ram. The ram holds his smile and keeps the gift baskets steady in his grip.

"Uh... can we help you?" asks Mortimer.

"Hello! I've got gift baskets for you!" blurts the ram, making Mortimer and Claribel flinch.

He steps off the elevator and looks around, whistling impressively.

"Wow. This place looks a lot cleaner than when I last saw it," says the ram. "I know Rolland's group didn't clean it. Who was it?"

He looks at Claribel.

"Was it you? It was you, wasn't it?" he says.

"Yeah..." says Claribel.

"Good job. Great job, actually! I love what you did with the place!"

"I'm sorry, but who are you?" asks Mortimer.

"I'm Ramsey Prosper," says the ram. "I am Mama Bear's cook for this region. I meant to drop these off yesterday, but after hearing what happened, I decided to wait for the mood to settle. By the way, the gift baskets are for you. Just reminding you."

Mortimer and Claribel holster their pistols and take the baskets. After setting them on the coffee table, Claribel immediately opens hers, and Mortimer returns to the kitchen, grabs the moose track pint, and starts eating it with his fingers while going back to the living room.

"Mortimer, right?" asks Ramsey, pointing at the fox.

Mortimer nods.

"I heard you had a run-in with the Hobo Warrior Bunny," says Ramsey.

"Who told you?"

"I went to Taco king for lunch, but Juarez had the place closed for repairs. He told me what happened. He also said you and the Hobo Warrior are banned from his restaurant."

"Please, it's not a restaurant. It's a fast-food joint. And since you're here, do you know anything that can help us get rid of the Hobo?"

"And Bazooka Bunny, too," says Claribel as she inspects an expensive bottle of scale cleaner.

"Ah, well, I'd like to help, but the Hobo Warrior Bunny is a mystery. He just appeared one day with a lust for violence. A scourge on the Mama Bear Syndicate, and every criminal making an honest living. As for the Bazooka Bunny? She has always been a part of Bliss Town. We just don't know where she lives. Or the Hobo for that matter."

Mortimer frowns at this, and Claribel holds her gift basket tightly.

"How about places of work? Does the Hobo have a favorite spot to wash windows?" asks Mortimer.

"Hobo just does whatever. Bums money, walks around, and hits our guys with his freaky stick like the douche bag he is," says Ramsey.

"Okay, what about the Bazooka chick?" asks Mortimer.

"Stella's Strip House, but only part time and that place is off limits for Mama Bear related work," says Ramsey.

"Why is that place off limits?" asks Mortimer.

"Ask Mama Bear."

Mortimer sighs heavily and rubs his brows. "You're really busting my balls here, big guy."

Ramsey shrugs. "Oh well."

"There's no way a part time stripper can afford bazookas and armor," says Claribel.

"I know, but we don't know what her second source of income is. And the thing is, is that we would have already gotten rid of the Hobo and Bazooka if we could, but we can't and Mama Bear didn't think the problem was bad enough to send Thaddeus and his posse, which is why she sent you two," says Ramsey.

Mortimer chuckles nervously. "Yeah, we don't need Thaddeus down here. We'll take care of this hobo and bazooka babe in no time. We've just been caught off guard about how determined they are to live."

"I'm assuming you and Rolland have thought of plans to kill those two. We'll need to know what they were so we can avoid them," says Claribel.

"Ah, that's the neat part. We haven't had a single plan!" says Ramsey.

Mortimer and Claribel stare at Ramsey with smoldering glares.

"What?" says Mortimer heavily.

Ramsey sits on the couch next to Claribel, prompting her to move down a couple of cushions.

"Originally we were hoping the Hobo Warrior and Bazooka Bunny would kill each other because their rivalry is just so intense, but it is taking too long," says Ramsey. "We were also hoping that the Hobo Warrior would die of food poisoning because he's always eating from the trash, but nothing makes that guy sick."

"Those are stupid plans," says Mortimer.

"We might have to go with the classic route and just overwhelm them in an ambush," says Claribel.

Mortimer rubs his chin. "Right..." He stops rubbing his chin and stiffens. "You're right! Clair, where's Rolland's group?"

"At the gym," replies Claribel.

"Thanks!"

Mortimer rushes out of the room, leaving his ice cream on the coffee table. Claribel and Ramsey are left alone, the ticking of a hidden clock being the only noise in the house. Ramsey runs his hands through his hair nervously as Claribel awkwardly avoids eye contact.

Suddenly, Mortimer barges back into the room, snatches his shoes, and slams the door shut once more, leaving Claribel and Ramsey in an awkward state. Seconds pass, and Ramsey takes a deep breath and looks at Claribel with a practiced smile.

"So... A snake, eh?" says Ramsey.

"Yeah..." says Claribel.

"I haven't seen one of you in a while."

"Neither have I."

"Right... Right... So, are you single?"

Claribel frowns and her tail rattles.

A Bad Day- 03

The brakes of the Paulie's Pillows truck grind as it slows to a stop at a red light. After it stops, there is a series of rapid bangs that get louder and harder with each passing second, causing the trailer to vibrate and the doors to bend. The truck's hazard lights turn on, and the driver, an old rabbit with gray fur and heavy glasses, hurries to the trailer doors.

He swears and stumbles back when the trailer breaks open. Pillows spill out as Jayson falls on the road with numerous pillows following behind him. Jayson is clutching his cosmic weapon, and he is covered in soot and blood.

"What in the world? Where did you come from?" says the driver.

"The sky," says Jayson.

The driver looks up at the cracked sky, and then at Jayson.

"No, you didn't," says the driver.

"Feel free not to believe me," says Jayson as he throws the pillows back in the trailer. When the last of the pillows are back inside, he closes the bent doors, and then goes to a nearby tree, breaks off a branch, and slides it between the door handles. After that, he walks away, leaving the driver confused.

"Uh... Thanks?" says the driver.

"No problem," says Jayson, giving a short farewell wave without looking at him.

Jayson continues walking, and the truck drives away. As Jayson walks, he sees a two-story, brick building with dirty windows and a faded mural of a muscular badger lifting two tons of weights. The sign says: "**BIG BODY BUDDY GYM**." It also has a *"For Sale"* sign taped to the window. But the best part is that it is on his side, so he doesn't have to worry about Lexia blowing him up with a rocket again.

Jayson inspects himself, noting the caked-on blood mixing with the grime of hobo life, and when he sniffs himself, he recoils with a wrinkled nose. He quickens his steps, leaving a wretched scent-trail of rot, sweat, and broken dreams.

Jayson enters the gym and looks around at the old wooden interior illuminated by failing lights. It has everything a gym needs: wrestling ring (in use), lines of weights (in use), fancy exercise machines (in use), yoga mats (in use), and tables, couches, and chairs (in use with gym members taking breathers). It doesn't take Jayson long to see Rolland (on a couch), with Dacre, Cyrus, and Shae at a table, playing One-O. They don't notice him, and Jayson doesn't care.

He goes straight to the complimentary showers, turns on the hot water at full blast, and steps inside, clothes and all. The water cascading off of him immediately turns into a sludge of brown, black, green, red, and orange. Gym goers stare at Jayson with a mix of curiosity and disgust as bubbles from their soap and steam from their showers strategically cover their male reproductive organs. The ones closest to Jayson move away from him as the sludge spreads and dirty speckles fly from the impacts of the hot water.

Jayson uses his fingers to claw out the gunk in his hair and scrape out the filth in his fabric, and when he is done, he shuts off the water and turns on a giant air dryer built into the wall. The hot air blows off the excess water, leading to more discolored liquid seeping off of him. His clothes become crusted on the outside and damp on the inside, while his hair and fur are frazzled, but he exits the shower feeling satisfied.

When Jayson reenters the gym lobby, he takes a deep breath, and walks towards the exit, but abruptly stops when he hears Rolland yelling out to him.

"Oi! What are you doing here, Hobo?"

Jayson looks to the side and sees Rolland and his group glaring at him, their One-O cards still in play.

"I had to take a shower. But don't worry, I'm going home now," says Jayson.

"Home? You ain't got a burrow. You're a hobo," says Rolland.

"Home is where the heart is."

"Says the heartless rabbit."

"Rich coming from the guy who kills hearts."

Rolland slams his cards into a block and sets them on the table, glaring at Jayson.

"You know this is our turf, right?" says Rolland.

"Really? I had no idea. But since I'm here, why don't you try teaching me a lesson. Unless you're scared," says Jayson.

Rolland narrows his eyes while Jayson approaches the group. When he is a few steps away, the thugs surround him, and Rolland glares at him while the others crack their knuckles or roll their necks.

"Are you going to go for it? Or are you going to give me twenty bucks?" says Jayson.

"How about we gun you down right here, right now?" says Rolland.

Jayson rubs his wooden sword's hilt. "Well, for starters, blood on the floor is not good. It is a pain in the ass to clean. You might as well replace the flooring. And a non-natural death can lower your property value anywhere from ten to twenty-five percent, not including the difficulty you would get selling the place due to the stigma that comes with murder properties. Then there's your afternoon being ruined where you have to transport my body to an appropriate area, dig a hole at least six feet deep, and then drop my body in said hole. Then cover the hole in such a way that the area looks undisturbed. On top of that, you need to make sure your witnesses are on the same page, and then it gets really tedious, because you have to keep an eye on them, and then one or more of your friends might snitch on you if they get pissed off enough. Giving me twenty bucks will be easier for all of us."

"I got a better idea. How about we take you to Ramsey and have him slit your throat and then put your body in a vat of acid and bury you somewhere in the desert?" says Rolland.

Jayson arches a brow. "Who's Ramsey?"

"None of your business."

"Oh, well, fine. I'll just leave then."

Jayson turns to leave, but Cyrus and Shae block him, and Rolland wags his finger at the Hobo Warrior Bunny.

"Oh no. You're not going anywhere. You gotta pay for the other night, and all the other nights. You've been a pain in the ass ever since you came from God-knows-where, and we're going to take care of this right now!"

Dacre raises his suppressed pistol. In a flash, the world dims. Jayson disarms Dacre and slams him into the table, shattering it.

Then Cyrus and Shae rush Jayson, and he draws his weapon at blinding speed. He is surrounded in the faint aura, and with time slowing down, he proceeds to disarm and viciously beat down Cyrus and Shae with intense speed.

During the chaos, Cyrus is thrown onto the floor and Shae is kicked into the wall. When Dacre gets up and attempts to shoot Jayson again, he is whacked out the window with a sonic boom that rattles the gym.

People scream and scatter, their bodies mere silhouettes in the darkness, and the Specter watches the scene unfold as Jayson turns to Rolland. His narrowed eyes focused on the thug.

As he marches forward, Rolland draws his pistol, but Jayson snatches a water bottle from a table and throws it at him, striking him in the face and causing him to miss his shot.

Jayson then charges and with a loud yell, he whacks Rolland across the gym, creating a dust and debris cloud when he hits the wall.

The dust settles several seconds later, revealing Rolland to be stuck in the wall. The world brightens immediately after, and Jayson smiles and walks away with his cosmic-wood sword resting against his shoulder. Rolland glares at Jayson from the wall, bloodied and bruised and eyes pulsing with pure rage.

"One day I'll get you, Hobo... One day," says Rolland.

Meanwhile, outside in the pleasant sunshine and warm breeze, Jayson walks past Dacre's unconscious and bloodied form and disappears into the alley.

Several seconds later, Mortimer rounds the corner, wearing his raccoon mask, and he sees Dacre on the sidewalk, surrounded by glass and splintered wood.

"You gotta be kidding me," grumbles Mortimer.

He enters the gym and sees the others knocked out and Rolland stuck in the wall. Mortimer runs up to Rolland and pulls him out. With his body now free, Rolland staggers and uses the fox for support as he winces and clutches his gut.

"Alright, spill it. What happened here?" says Mortimer.

"The Hobo came by to take a shower and beat us up for no reason," says Rolland.

"Can you walk?"

"If you inject me with something or let me snort something, then yeah."

"Good. Wake up your gang. We're going after the Hobo Warrior Bunny."

"How? He's practically demonic."

"Simple. We overwhelm him, then kill him. Then we'll do the same for Bazooka Bunny."

Rolland rolls his eyes. "Oh wow. Such a brilliant, glorious plan. How could we have never thought of such a wonderful, flawless plan? You must have the IQ of a god!"

Mortimer grabs Rolland by the neck and slams him into the wall, making the rabbit wince again.

"Rolland don't start with me," snarls Mortimer, pointing at his nose with his claw. "Get your group, have them get their friends, and meet me... Where's a good place to meet?"

"The Toxic War monument on Sixth Street and Harper Drive," says Rolland.

"Good. Meet me there in four hours. That should be more than enough time to get everyone. Then we're going to get the Hobo Warrior Bunny."

"How? Do you have specifics besides mob him?"

Mortimer releases Rolland and smiles proudly behind his mask while clasping the flaps of his jacket, all while Rolland rubs his neck and glares at the fox.

"Ah, allow me to explain my plan in great detail," says Mortimer. "You see, the first thing we do is—"

A Bad Day- 04

Endless water ripples from the heavy thumps in a dark world. Light pours through a clock-shaped crack in the near-black sky, and the cracks shift like a clock hand telling time. Each shift brings a haunting thump, causing the lukewarm water to tremble and the reflections in the water to break from the ripples.

"Jayson..." hums a female, her voice honeyed and floating through the air.

Jayson's eyes and ears twitch and strain for the female, and he paces in circles, searching for the one calling him. The thumping from the clock-shaped cracks is like a hammer and chisel to his ears, and the ankle-deep water splashes about as he paces. He puts on a brave face, but his chest is tight from his racing heart.

"Why are you afraid, Jayson?" asks the female, her voice in his ears despite her not being near him.

Jayson continues to pace, stopping when he sees the nearly all-black specter rising from the water twenty feet from him. Her body is lanky, covered by torn clothing with two red lines on her wrists, following her arm straight to the elbow. The torn fabric and long black hair floats in the air as if submerged in water. White voids for eyes stare at Jayson while the figure's face splits open, revealing the white pit for her mouth.

"Don't you want to see again?" asks the Specter.

Jayson's eyes widen and his ears droop. "What are you?"

"You know who I am."

"No, I don't."

"It's me. Lexanne. The one you loved long ago."

Jayson shakes his head and steps back. "You're not Lexanne."

"Oh really? Maybe this will refresh your memory."

The Specter extends her hands and turns them so Jayson can see the red marks going up to her elbows, each pumping out red liquid that splatters in the water and spreads outward, carried by the ripples. Her grin widens, nearly ripping her head in half.

"Come see with me," *she says.*

(((***)))

Jayson jolts awake on a public bench, shaking and sweating as the late afternoon sun heats him up. Nearby are a pair of dirty and ragged rabbits, giggling and twitching with dilated eyes.

Jayson stares at them, but they don't notice him. Then Jayson sees a twenty-buck bill lying on the ground. He stares at it. It stays put. He sits up and reaches for it, but it is pulled away by a fishing wire taped to it.

Jayson frowns and holds his cosmic weapon tight.

"Really? You guys thought I was going to fall for that?" says Jayson.

"I told you it was a stupid plan," says Rolland, his body hidden but his voice easy to hear, despite him trying to whisper.

"Shut up. It was perfect in every way," snaps Mortimer. Then he yells, "Get him, boys!"

There are multiple clicks, an engine revs and tires screech, and Jayson's eyes widen.

A van speeds around the corner with its side door open, and rabbits wearing ski masks, armed with Uzis and pistols, aim at Jayson.

Time slows as Jayson draws his weapon, creating the aura around him. Bullets fly, and Jayson's eyes narrow while the world darkens around him. Jayson screams and charges the van while the junkies are gunned down, dying laughing.

Jayson is pierced by bullets, but he pays no attention as he swings his cosmic weapon at the van. A powerful shock wave emanates from the impact and the bubble of time manipulation expands around him.

The van crumbles and its windows shatter as it flies through the air, its broken body, loose fragments, and flailing thugs twirling seconds slower than the world outside. When the destroyed vehicle and airborne thugs exit the time dilation, their bouncing becomes fast and jarring.

The van rolls across the street and collides with a lamppost. The loose thugs hit the ground with loud crunches and their bloody, twisted bodies become still.

A pair of thugs groan and try to crawl out, but they vanish in a flash of fire and rubble when a rocket strikes the van.

"Ha! Killtacular!" shouts Lexia from her perch on the roof, clutching her bazooka.

Blood pours from Jayson's wounds, and he runs to Lexia's side while Rolland's group comes out of hiding, brandishing shotguns. They aim their weapons at Jayson, but Lexia shoots a rocket at them, forcing them to scatter.

The rocket hits the sidewalk, flinging broken concrete bits into the sky. Then Jayson changes course and charges the nearest member of Rolland's group: Shae.

"Are we doing this again!" shouts Jayson.

He hits Shae through a nearby window, and he ducks and rolls, leaving thick droplets of blood on the ground as Dacre tries shooting him. And while this happens, Lexia jumps off the roof and lands on a car, breaking its windows.

Jayson's clothes are wet with blood as he rushes Dacre and engages him, all while Cyrus aims his shotgun at him. But before he can shoot, Lexia bolts towards him and does a leaping kick to his head.

Cyrus flies off his feet and hits a car. He slumps down with his teeth broken and blood pooling out of his mouth, all while Jayson beats down Dacre.

After Dacre is beaten into submission, Jayson stumbles with thicker blood droplets dotting the pavement, and he and Rolland lock eyes. Jayson's heartbeat and breathing become heavier, his eyes narrow, and everything goes darker as he focuses on Rolland.

Behind him is Lexanne, standing in the shadows, her presence known only because of the white eyes staring at Jayson.

"You little turds are on my side now!" yells Lexia, her voice faint.

"Come see with me," calls Lexanne.

Rolland aims his shotgun at Jayson, and Jayson legs stumble as he rushes forward. He yells and whacks the shotgun down as Rolland fires, breaking bits of the road, and then he swiftly hits the thug.

Rolland sails through the air, breaking through the upper window of a two-story building. And then a bullet rips through Jayson's back and Lexia is shot multiple times.

Jayson and Lexia drop to the ground, and Mortimer walks through Lexanne, reloading a pistol while Jayson coughs blood and shifts around, his body becoming slick and weak.

"Well, that did not go nearly as well as I had hoped," says Mortimer.

Lexia suddenly rolls to her feet and draws her pistol and a knife, and Jayson uses his weapon to prop himself on his knees while clutching one of his many wounds.

"Ha! I'm wearing armor!" says Lexia.

Mortimer groans. "Ah shit. I thought you were cosplaying as an Amazonian princess. You certainly fit the part."

Lexia smiles brightly with hearts in her eyes. "Awww... Thank you!"

Mortimer grimaces and Jayson tries to stand, but falls to his knees, his blue clothing now almost completely red, and the white fur on his muzzle dripping blood.

"Lexia, he's trying to kill us!" says Jayson.

"But he complimented me," says Lexia.

Mortimer aims his pistol at Lexia's head.

"I'm just being polite before I kill you two," says Mortimer.

Jayson growls and rushes Mortimer in a blur of speed. He whacks the pistol out of Mortimer's hand, and when he goes for another strike, Mortimer dodges and uses Jayson's momentum to throw him into a brick wall. Jayson falls with blood all around him.

Then Mortimer dodges Lexia's shots, snatches his pistol off the ground, and returns fire.

Incredibly inaccurate bullets whizz past Mortimer and Lexia as they run and shoot, breaking glass, popping tires, and ricocheting off the ground or lamp posts.

Mortimer and Lexia slide to cover on opposite sides of the same parked car, both reloading their pistols. After they reload, Mortimer slides around and attempts to shoot Lexia again, but she diverts the shot by slicing his arm with her knife.

When Lexia tries shooting Mortimer, he dodges, draws a knife from his back sheath and attempts to slash her.

Lexia barely blocks and stumbles back while Mortimer aims his pistol. She sloppily dodges Mortimer's shot, quickly recovers her footing, and the two go at it again.

Slash, deflect, shoot, deflect, slash, deflect. Blocking, kicking, slashing, shooting. It is a mess with every thunderous gunshot making Jayson's ears ring.

And Jayson is still on the ground, clutching his wounds and crawling towards his cosmic-wood sword, leaving a trail of blood in his wake.

Meanwhile, Lexia and Mortimer go in circles with their attacks, blocks, and counterattacks, but Jayson's world gets darker. Lexanne appears again, holding her bloody hand out to Jayson.

"Come on, Jayson. Come see with me," says Lexanne.

Jayson grits his teeth, blood and sweat soak his body. "I can't."

"You will."

Suddenly, there is a blast of a loud gunshot and Mortimer is knocked off his feet. In the distance, sirens and police lights are rapidly approaching.

Lexia, who is panting and covered with a fresh collection of cuts, looks around, and then up, and steps back. Derrick lands near Jayson and scoops up him and his weapon.

"Meet me at my nest," orders Derrick.

Derrick flies away, and Lexia immediately runs after him.

*****

Mortimer winces and rolls on his hands and knees, and he checks himself. Blood drips from his cuts and a bullet wound. He rips open his shirt and sees a bullet stuck in his vest, but its tip still punctured him. Mortimer glares down the alley and sees Lexia rounding a corner, and he looks to where Jayson was and sees a black feather sitting in the blood.

Mortimer grabs it, looks at the sky, and when he sees red and blue lights reflecting off the buildings, he hobbles away, disappearing from view right as police cars swerve into the carnage.

Cops jump out and immediately begin cuffing Shae, Dacre, and Cryus, and a firetruck works on putting out the fire from the van Lexia blew up.

****

Meanwhile, in a nearby diner known as Klumsy K's, Trafford Augustine is sitting at a table that gives him a clear view of everything that happened. The patrons are casually eating and drinking their food, uncaring of the carnage outside, while Trafford watches with interest. He is so engrossed in the spectacle that he doesn't notice Mariana Cross approaching him, wearing the cafe waitress uniform, and holding his bill.

"Don't worry. This is a daily thing," says Mariana.

"Neat," says Trafford.

"No, it's not. Here's your bill."

Mariana drops the bill next to Trafford's empty plate and leaves.

Trafford looks at the bill, shrugs, drops the appropriate amount of money on the table, and leaves without giving her a tip. Once outside, Trafford watches the police shove Rolland's men into their police cars while another pair drag Rolland out of the building he was whacked into. More cops fan out to search the area. This brings him to smile and pull out his notebook.

"What an interesting place," says Trafford.

A Bad Day- 05

Several hours after the failed ambush, Rolland, Cyrus, Dacre, and Shae are stuck in a jail cell, all bloody and bruised. A pair of cops sit at a nearby table, with one reading newspapers marked with a headline saying: *"MAYOR MARCOS MACANAS & GOV GALTERO GARCIAGUIRADO WIN RE-ELECTIONS IN EARLY MORNING LANDSLIDE VICTORIES!"*

The other cop is playing a crossword puzzle game that came from the newspaper.

"Hey, what's the study of ancient species?" asks the cop with the crossword puzzle.

"Nerdology," says the one with the newspaper dismissively.

Then a crackling buzz blurts out from the speaker overhead, and the metal door sealing the occupants inside opens. Claribel enters soon after with Mariana Cross in a police uniform as an escort. Claribel is unarmed, while Mariana has a pistol clipped to her hip.

The cops stare at Claribel with some confusion and wonder, but she ignores them and goes to the jail cell while Mariana unlocks it. Rolland is the first to leave, but he stops when Claribel pokes him in the chest.

"You're lucky the bail laws are generous," says Claribel.

"You call it lucky, but Mama Bear calls it investing in local resources. Now I'm ready to go home," says Rolland.

****

Back at the safehouse, Mortimer is sitting in a chair in the dining room, bandaged and drinking lemonade. Beneath the chair are torn garbage bags to make sheets to cover the floor and table, and Ramsey is washing his bloody hands in the sink. Mortimer's vest is resting on top of a plastic sheet, and his bloody clothes are in the trash.

"You're lucky you wore that vest. That bullet would have gutted you," says Ramsey.

"I never leave without it. But a bird shot me, and I want to know who it was," says Mortimer.

Ramsey goes to the cabinet, opens it, and is momentarily stunned when he sees everything is organized by type and in alphabetical order. But after a few seconds of his eyes darting around, he finds his protein cookies, and takes them to Mortimer.

"What kind of bird are we talking about?" asks Ramsey while giving Mortimer the small round pastries.

Mortimer thanks him, bites into one, and his chewing shifts from a glimmer of happiness to confusion, then to disgust. He inspects the cookie, noting that it looks like a chocolate chip cookie, but tastes like cardboard soaked in old hamburger fat.

"What's wrong with this cookie?" asks Mortimer.

"It's a protein cookie. Now, what about the bird?"

Mortimer sets the cookies down and chugs his lemonade. Once the cup is empty, he puts it on the table, rim side down.

"I'm not sure, to be honest. I didn't see who shot me, but it was from an odd angle that only a bird can pull off," says Mortimer. He pulls out the black feather from his pocket and gives it to Ramsey. "This is where you come in. Work your science magic and find out what this guy is."

****

"*Come see with me.*"

Jayson wakes up with a start, covered in bandages and laying in Derrick's nest of pillows, cushions, and blankets. He looks outside and sees Derrick sitting on the porch. Then he looks to the side and sees Lexia cleaning her homemade bazooka in the dining room. She is also covered in bandages.

"What happened?" asks Jayson groggily.

"Derrick shot the fox," says Lexia.

"That's a relief. That ambush... I wasn't expecting that," says Jayson.

"Yeah, that's generally how ambushes work. And you're lucky Derrick showed up because I would have just let you bleed to death."

"Always the charmer."

Lexia slides her weapon aside and looks at Jayson, holding a stern expression with glazed eyes.

"I'm serious. One hundred percent would have left you to die," says Lexia.

Jayson stares at Lexia, and she stares back at him. She is still frowning and blinking the wetness out of her eyes, and he isn't shy about his annoyance being written all over his face.

"You know, one of these days you'll have to explain why you're a prickly cactus to me," says Jayson.

Lexia resumes cleaning her rocket launcher, and Derrick walks in, goes to the fridge, and grabs a small bottle of orange juice.

"I didn't see anyone, but I have my sensors ready, so if anyone shows up, we'll know in advance," says Derrick. He goes to Jayson and gives him the orange juice. "How're you feeling?"

"Good. Which is surprising, considering how many times I was shot," says Jayson as he opens his orange juice.

"I used some leftover medijects from my time in the Toxic War. Heals wounds quickly. Unfortunately, you lost a good amount of blood, so you're going to have to take it easy for a bit."

"So, easy as in...?"

"Lexia will take over things while you recover."

Lexia fist-pumps. "Yes!"

Derrick glares at Lexia, and she smiles nervously.

"I mean... Happy to help," says Lexia.

"That's better," says Derrick.

He then pats Jayson's head and turns on the TV. The TV has a third person view of a video game character of a female mouse wearing an explorer outfit traversing a blocky jungle with blocky water and blocky rocks and blocky ruins. At the corner of the screen is pixelated "GSC."

"I'm going to make dinner. You two relax and behave yourselves," says Derrick.

And coming from the TV is an obnoxiously fake-happy narrator. *"Helllloooo, everybody! Game Streaming Channel presents, Ms. Fritz Bee! Aaaaaand... her favorite game, Block World! Disclaimer: AllfootageisprerecordedthreeweeksinadvanceandallfootageiseditedbyprofessionalsthereforeitisitechnicallynotstreamingbutstreamingisacoolwordifyouwouldliketoenlistinGSCthenbuyourcatalogueandsignthe stuff.* **NOW IT'S GAME TIME!***"*

Lexia gasps and takes a flying leap on the couch, and Jayson uses his cosmic-wood sword as a cane to go to the couch. He sits next to Lexia, and the harlequin-hare's brown eyes sparkle as she focuses on the screen.

"Oh, Block World! I love Block World! And Ms. Fritz Bee is the best Block World player! I would love to have her autograph," Lexia squees. "I wonder what the challenge is going to be today. I hope it's a civilization run. Those are always fun."

Jayson rolls his eyes and Lexia turns up the volume.

"Hello, everyone! It's me, Ms. Fritz Bee, for another episode of Block World," says the player, her voice carrying a slight South Welsh accent. *"Today's challenge is going to be creating a civilization with three hundred other players! We're going to do it colonial style."*

"Yes! I love it when they do these civilization scenario things! They're always goofy! My favorite is when they do sword and sorcery civilizations. That's when things really get nutty."

Jayson reaches for the remote, but Lexia slaps his hand.

"No! Bad!" says Lexia.

"But the Xenia marathon is on," says Jayson.

"How do you know?"

"Call it a hunch."

"Not good enough." Lexia sits on top of the remote. "My remote now. Unless you want to dig for it."

Jayson sighs heavily. "No. I'll let you have the remote, but I call dibs on it in an hour."

"Bull. Nobody uses dibs."

"I use dibs."

"Since when?"

"Since now. And since I called dibs, that means you have to give me the remote in an hour," says Jayson.

"You have to actually spot it first to mark it for dibs, Jayson!" says Lexia.

Jayson's hand shoots forward with the speed of a viper and he snatches the remote out from underneath Lexia's hip with impressive accuracy. Lexia is stunned, her expression a mix of surprise and embarrassment as her face heats up. On the other hand, Jayson is smugly satisfied, having pulled off such an audacious maneuver, a mischievous smirk playing on his lips as he proudly holds up his trophy.

"Dibs on this remote in one hour," says Jayson.

He tosses the remote on Lexia's lap and relaxes on the couch, and Lexia's blush remains. Her wide eyes stay on Jayson for a few seconds before she turns to Derrick and points accusingly at Jayson.

"Derrick, Jayson cheated on dibs!" she cries out.

"Did not!" protests Jayson.

"He called dibs and both of you saw the remote after you tried hogging it, Lexia. Fair's fair," says Derrick without looking at them.

Lexia glares daggers at Jayson, who grins back in amusement. Derrick, however, is busy rummaging through his freezer and pulls out a rather suspicious frosty box with a slice of blueberry pie pictured on it.

"Do you two want this blueberry pie?" asks Derrick.

Jayson and Lexia exchange an awkward glance before they both respond to the offer in unison.

"Sure!" says Jayson.

Lexia insists, "Yes please!"

Derrick sets the oven to preheat, and then quietly goes about preparing dinner. And Jayson and Lexia watch Ms. Fritz Bee traverse the dangerous environment of *Block World* in total silence. But when Lexia puts up a cushion wall between her and Jayson, he smirks, adjusts his position, and presses his feet against her wall while resting against the arm of the couch, locking her in. Lexia growls, but Jayson doesn't budge. Despite getting shot to hell and losing a lot of blood, Jayson finds this moment a perfect way to end his day.

III

Relaxation

After getting shot by Mortimer, Jayson tries yet again to relax. However, Lexia doesn't know what relaxation is, and Mortimer is still trying to kill him.

III

Relaxation- 01

A comforting golden hue from the civil dawn's light covers the dying city of Bliss Town. Most of the citizens are asleep or barely waking, and Jayson Hopper is no exception.

He is on the verge of passing out in his hiding spot behind a thicket of bushes. Staying crouched, his blue eyes, heavy with fatigue and framed by dark circles, remain fixed on the Taco King's battered green dumpster across the street. The chill of the morning air seeps through his dark blue jacket, making him shiver. His stomach growls incessantly. He licks his dry lips, yearning for the delicious trash burritos that wait in the dumpster.

Jayson watches Juarez stomp across the parking lot, cursing up a storm under his breath with a hefty bag of garbage in his hands. He flings his garbage into the dumpster and storms off without a second thought.

Once Juarez is back inside, Jayson sprints towards the refuse container, climbs up the lone wall guarding it, and dives headfirst into the mess, creating a cacophony of clattering cans and crinkling wrappers.

A few minutes later, Jayson erupts from the dumpster, clutching a bag of partially devoured food. With a whoop of triumph and eccentric cackling, he makes his speedy getaway to the neighboring park.

As Jayson sprints through the public patch of land, a net suddenly whooshes towards him. He curses and performs an impromptu leap, leading to a narrow escape from the net's clutches.

Before he can catch his breath, another net zooms towards him. Jayson swiftly pivots away from it, and as this happens, he hears Lexia's colorful stream of curses echoing in the empty park, prompting him to sprint off with renewed vigor, leading to pulses of pain throughout his body.

Loud thuds echo behind him, and as he glances back, his eyes widen in disbelief at the sight of the harlequin-hare barreling towards him. She's decked out in her homemade armor, a determined gleam in her eyes and her brawny limbs propelling her forward. Her snarl reveals a set of teeth as she gains momentum, sending patches of moist dead grass flying into the air with each forceful stride.

"Jayson! Get back here!" yells Lexia.

"Bite me!" shouts Jayson defiantly.

Lexia reaches behind her back and yanks out a boomerang decorated with sharp teeth and angry eyes. She keeps running, and her arm flexes as she preps the throw.

"Ah, crud," says Jayson.

He runs faster, bringing his wounds to throb with more intensity, and Lexia flings her boomerang. Jayson ducks as it whizzes by, nearly striking him in the head and causing him to stumble.

But that moment of slowness allows Lexia to put power into her legs, take a flying leap, and kick Jayson in the back.

His face crashes into the grass, and Lexia keeps steady on top of him as she rides him like a surfboard. By the time they are done sliding, there is a trail of destroyed brown grass. Jayson's groan is muffled by the plants in his mouth, and Lexia is panting with a proud smile.

"Ha! Gotcha! Now, where do you want to get bit?" says Lexia.

The boomerang suddenly hits Lexia on the side of the head, knocking her off Jayson.

"Ow! Son of a— God dang it, that hurts!" cries Lexia, laying on her back next to Jayson and holding her cheek.

"Serves you right," says Jayson, his face still in the grass.

Lexia slams her fist on the back of Jayson's head, causing him to grunt painfully. Then Lexia rolls on top of Jayson and digs her knee into his back while pulling out a roll of rope from her belt.

Jayson squirms, but Lexia keeps him pinned.

"What are you doing?" says Jayson.

RELAXATION- 01

Lexia's brawny limbs keep Jayson pinned as her large hands expertly work the rope to bind him with intricate knots. Each movement showcases a surprising nimbleness and dexterity that Jayson didn't realize she had. Soon, he finds himself immobilized in a hogtie.

Jayson grunts and wiggles on the ground, and Lexia stands up and smirks as she brushes her palms together.

"There we go. Nice and helpless," says Lexia.

"Okay, what gives?" says Jayson. "Taco King is my territory, so you have no right to do this!"

Lexia crouches in front of Jayson and smirks.

"Derrick said for you to take it easy. I saw you hopping around in the trash; therefore, you were exerting yourself in direct violation of Derrick's instructions. So, me being the good friend I am, put a stop to your self-destructive behavior," says Lexia with obnoxiously sweet affection.

Jayson groans. "You've got to be kidding me. Lexia, I'm always in that dumpster!"

"Yeah, and climbing counts as exertion," says Lexia. "So, I'm going to make sure you don't move. This will ensure that you obey Derrick and that I can clean up Bliss Town without interference... Now, where do you live?"

Jayson cocks a brow. "You don't know where I live?"

"How am I supposed to know where you live?" snaps Lexia.

"I'll give you a hint. Trees of green and red roses, too."

"Do you have any idea how little that narrows it down?"

"I guess you'll have to let me go, then. Shame. I was looking forward to company with a Wrestle World reject."

"Ha. Ha." Lexia tugs on the rope, tightening it and making Jayson wince. "Save us the trouble and tell me where you live."

"Only if you tell me where you live," says Jayson.

"Absolutely not."

"Then we're at an impasse."

"Impasse this!"

Lexia stomps on Jayson's head, knocking him into darkness.

Relaxation- 02

Jayson stands in the middle of the endless dark water. Light pours through the clock-shaped cracks in the sky and the cracks shift like a clock hand telling time, with each shift bringing thumps that ripple the water.

In front of Jayson is a white bathroom door. Water gurgles beyond it, and Jayson's ears perk. All he feels is panic as he runs to it; there are no words, no thoughts, just a drive to get through the door.

When he reaches it, he tries opening it, but it won't budge. He rattles the knob, bangs on it, kicks it, punches it, and when he breaks through by ramming his shoulder against it, he stumbles into a destroyed living room, dimly lit with broken furniture. A wedding dress is smoldering in a fireplace, and pictures lay broken on the floor.

Lexanne hums and her figure shifts in the darkness in front of Jayson.

"You came back," *says Lexanne.*

Jayson's eyes widen, and Lexanne grins and extends her bloody hands to him.

"Come see with me," *says Lexanne.*

(((***)))

Jayson's eyes snap open, and he finds he is no longer hogtied, but he is still wrapped in rope and is now being dragged through the forest by his legs, leaving a trail of dirt as his body pushes aside fallen leaves and twigs. Every now and then, orange and red leaves fall loose from the towering trees above them, showing a little bit more of the cracked sky past the canopy.

Meanwhile. Lexia has her rope over her shoulder. The leaves and twigs crunch under her heavy boots, her bazooka is strapped to her back, and she is muttering to herself as she looks around.

"Lexia, what are you doing?" says Jayson.

"Putting you out of the way of temptation and harm. Now, if I were a hobo, where would I be? Oh, yeah! At a homeless shelter like a normal bum!" says Lexia.

"I'm not normal."

"I know you're not normal!"

"You're not normal, either."

"I'm very normal!"

"Deny it all you want, but you're a freak, like me."

Lexia stops, drops the rope, and glares at Jayson with a fire in her twitching eye and her rocket aimed at him. Jayson's ears instantly droop, and his eyes get beady.

"But a good freak. The kind that everyone loves! Like goths! They're weird and everyone loves them!" says Jayson.

"Not everyone likes goths, Jayson," sneers Lexia.

"Everyone wants a goth girlfriend, Lexia."

"Lies and deceit!"

Lexia pulls the trigger and Jayson is blinded by a bright flash of light. He feels nothing, hears only ringing, and when his eyes flutter open, he finds himself lying in a ring of burnt leaves and the rope destroyed.

Then the pain comes rushing in, like molten lava consuming him. All he can do is seethe and twitch, and Lexia stands at the edge of the ring and blows the smoke out of her bazooka's barrel.

"You took that personally," says Jayson, his voice strained and his hand gradually sliding to his cosmic-wood sword's handle.

Lexia rolls her eyes with a scoff and clips her weapon on her back. "Did not. And don't be such a crybaby. That was a non-lethal rocket."

In a blink, Jayson springs up and yanks out his cosmic weapon, engulfing the area in a light blue hue. Time crawls, and all Lexia can do is widen her eyes as Jayson's wooden sword hits her in the abdomen.

Lexia flies back, and when she exits the bubble, she launches full speed away from Jayson. There is a loud crack in the air, and the mulch and weak branches are blown back while Lexia falls down a small hill, putting her out of sight.

Jayson falls to his knees, panting heavily from throbbing pain and a heavy heart. He is also grinning in Lexia's direction as he uses his weapon to keep him propped up.

"How'd you like that?" says Jayson.

At first there is silence. But that silence is broken when a chainsaw revs, and Jayson's smile drops. Lexia stomps into view seconds later, seething and tightly gripping a red chainsaw.

She revs the tool, and Jayson's eye twitches while his brain becomes clogged with mental smoke as it struggles to process what he is seeing. But so far, all he can muster is...

"Uh... What'cha got there, Lexia?" asks Jayson.

"My chainsaw. CHAINING TATUM!" yells Lexia.

Then she charges Jayson, and he curses up a storm and bolts through the forest. And Lexia cackles and runs after him while swinging her chainsaw madly.

****

Late morning light shines through Derrick's glass patio door, bathing him in tranquil warmth. Held between his talons is a miniature space soldier in bulky armor armed with a large weapon. In his other hand is a fine-tip, precision paintbrush, coating the gray plastic figure in blue. On the table, sitting on wax paper, are a dozen more of the figurines, all fully painted in blue, white, and gold colors. And next to him are all the brushes, paints, protective coatings, and airbrushes one needs for precise painting.

While Derrick paints his soldier, a female eagle wearing the blue uniform of a postal worker gracefully lands on his porch, carrying a mail bag. She raps on his glass door, and he stops painting. Slowly looks up. Then turns around and frowns. The female eagle, Bridgette Baggs, waves.

When Derrick opens the door, he hears faint chainsaw sounds and screams in the distance, but Bridgette doesn't seem to notice.

"Hello, Derrick! I got a delivery for you!" says Bridgette cheerfully.

Bridgette pulls out a wrapped box marked with "*Battle Hammer 401k.*" She gives it to Derrick. He takes it but looks past her shoulder with scrunched brows.

"Do you hear something?" asks Derrick.

"Oh, that chainsaw and screaming? Yeah, it's that Bazooka Bunny chasing the Hobo Warrior Bunny with a chainsaw," says Bridgette.

Derrick's eyes bulge.

"Honestly, they should just kiss already. I can see the tension from two miles away." Bridgette holds a form on a clipboard out to Derrick. "Sign here, please."

Derrick quickly signs the form, he slams the door in Bridgette's face, drops the case on his chair, and grabs his rifle.

"That girl's gonna be the death of me," grumbles Derrick.

****

Jayson slides behind a tree, hyperventilating and heart racing. The heavy thumps rapidly approach, and leaves and dirt are kicked up when Lexia slides next to him with a manic smile.

"TIME TO RELAX, JAYSON!" yells Lexia.

Jayson screams and Lexia swipes at him. Jayson blocks the chainsaw with his cosmic weapon, and then hits Lexia away.

Lexia flies off her feet, and she bounces and skids across the ground, leaving a gash in the mulch. When she stops, her face is in the ground, her body is twitching, and a growl rumbles from her throat while her chainsaw lays a few paces away from her grip.

"Lexia, enough! I can't relax if you're chasing me with a chainsaw!" says Jayson.

Lexia pushes herself up, snatches her chainsaw off the ground, and revs it again.

"I just want to bite you with my chainsaw!" says Lexia.

Lexia races towards Jayson, and he curses and resumes running.

"You're crazy! You're super crazy, Lexia!" yells Jayson.

****

In a peaceful, untainted portion of the forest, camp gear is set up on a small clearing, and Mortimer, wearing his raccoon mask, smiles and rubs his hands together as he stares at the beautiful orange, red, and brown hues of autumn leaves high above him.

"This is an excellent camping spot. With Ramsey's information, we should be able to find our target," says Mortimer to himself. He takes a deep breath and looks up at the sky with a smile. "It's almost over."

«<O»>

Mortimer is in his bedroom, doing push-ups with one hand, muscles rippling and his gorgeous un-scarred face staring at the wall filled with praises of jobs well done, best magician ever, and everyone adoring him. Behind him is a wall of high-tech computer equipment, all beeping and displaying colorful lights and streams of data that he reads as easily as a children's alphabet book.

The door opens, and Ramsey slides in, his black shirt tight against his bulging muscles, and his white lab coat barely fits him.

"Mortimer Walters," says Ramsey.

"Ramsey Prosper," says Mortimer.

Mortimer springs to his feet and the two shake hands, muscles flexing, their eyes magnetized to each other's awesomeness.

Ramsey holds up a filthy black feather, plagued with neglect and self-loathing.

"This feather belongs to a bald eagle," says Ramsey.

Mortimer snatches the feather and inspects it with pure sleuthing mastery.

"Excellent. I trust you know where bald eagles live. After all, I'm not from around here," says Mortimer.

"There's an enclave of them at the edge of Bliss Town," says Ramsey.

"Good." Mortimer clenches his fist, crushing the feather. "As Mama Bear's bestest Fixer, I will go there with my super-hot future wife and kill the Hobo Warrior Bunny

and his eagle friend once and for all. Claribel!"

Claribel slides in, wearing a form-fitting all-black outfit with a large leather coat and dark sunglasses. Her golden hair is pulled tight into a ponytail, and she is holding two SMGs in her hands.

"Yes, my love?" says Claribel.

"Time to save our world from the Hobo," says Mortimer.

"Excellent choice, my love."

Then the two run out of the house, jump on a pair of motorcycles, and zoom away towards a dark forest with large, winding trees and sharp thorny bushes. All while Ramsey stands on the roof with a single high-testosterone tear trailing his cheek.

"Godspeed, brave ones," whispers Ramsey.

«<O»>

Mortimer smiles whimsically with his hands on his hips and his gaze turned to the fluffy clouds partially blocking the cracked sky.

"Yes... Beautiful moment," says Mortimer quietly. He exhales after that, claps his hands, and turns sharply on his heels to smile at his future wife. "Claribel, darling, how are you doing?"

Claribel screams furiously and tugs at her blonde hair. Her tail rattles and the tent lays in shambles at her feet, with her hat, and rifle resting on a nearby rock.

"This sucks!" cries Claribel. "How do tents work? Why are they this complicated?" With frazzled hair and a twitching eye, she holds up a bent metal pole shoved inside another bent metal pole. "And why do these metal thingies never fit?"

Mortimer sighs heavily and approaches the mess. He firmly grabs Claribel's shoulders and guides her to sit on the rock with her Stetson hat and rifle.

"Why don't you have a seat while I put up the tent," says Mortimer.

Claribel looks down, grumbling and folding her arms tightly, and Mortimer snatches a couple pieces and inspects them. But while inspecting them, his ears twitch at the faint ruckus of a chainsaw and screams. Claribel notices this too, and they look in the direction of the noise.

Said noise is rapidly approaching.

"What is that?" wonders Mortimer.

Claribel puts on her hat, grabs her rifle, and checks it while the chainsaw and screams get louder. Then suddenly, Jayson jumps through some bushes with Lexia trailing him with a chainsaw and a wide grin.

"Oh crud!" shouts Mortimer, reeling back.

Claribel shrieks and falls on her butt as she backpedals.

"You wanted me to bite you, Jayson! Remember!" screams Lexia.

"Not literally!" snaps Jayson.

Jayson slides behind Mortimer and uses him as a shield, tugging him in every direction he can to keep Lexia from whacking him. This puts both of them in a circle, and Mortimer holds his hands up while darting his focus between Lexia and Jayson.

"What is going on!? Don't use me as a shield!" yells Mortimer.

"It'll be just for a second!" says Jayson desperately.

Claribel shoots the chainsaw out of Lexia's hands, and Mortimer snaps around and tackles Jayson to the ground before he can draw his weapon.

Jayson quickly kicks Mortimer off and clutches his side as he rolls over and stumbles back to his feet.

Lexia draws her knife and jumps to cover as Claribel continues shooting at her.

"Jayson, it's those Fixers!" says Lexia.

"No shit, Hopperinicus!" snaps Jayson.

Mortimer draws his knife and swipes at Jayson. The Hobo Warrior draws his cosmic weapon and easily blocks the swipes, taking quick and calculated steps back as the fox pushes forward.

A few blocks later, Jayson hits Mortimer, and the Fixer skids across the forest ground, falls off a drop, and lands in a bush.

With Mortimer out of sight, Jayson kneels and clutches his side again, breathing heavily.

As this happens, Claribel rushes Lexia. Lexia grabs the rifle and swings Claribel into the tree. Claribel's tail wraps around Lexia's leg and tugs her down.

Lexia falls, but keeps her grip on Claribel's rifle, causing both crash to the ground and roll over each other, cursing and making high-pitched yells as they battle for dominance.

While they roll around, Jayson grits his teeth, runs to Claribel, and hits her with his weapon, creating a burst of energy. Claribel flies in the air and lands in a nearby creek. The water splashes, and Claribel is motionless as she floats away.

Lexia and Jayson watch the current carry the rattlesnake away, and once she goes around a curve, Lexia smiles at Jayson.

"Wow. Great teamwork," says Lexia. She holds out her fist. "Pound it."

Jayson glares at Lexia, panting heavily and clutching his throbbing side. A few more seconds of tense silence pass before Derrick lands near them and stomps forward, eyes burning and the world darkening around him.

"Alright, what's going on here?" says Derrick.

Jayson points at Lexia. "Lexia chased me with a chainsaw!"

Lexia scoffs. "Tattle tale. Also, the chainsaw was harmless."

She points at the shot tool, and Derrick and Jayson look at it, seeing that there is no cutting chain on the guide bar. Derrick and Jayson turn their smoldering gazes to Lexia, and she smiles nervously and takes a step back, while drumming her fingers together.

"Alright, hear me out…" says Lexia.

Then she runs away and dives off a drop.

Relaxation- 03

Jayson and Derrick watch Lexia disappear into the surrounding tree as she runs through the forest, leaving a trail of kicked-up leaves and twigs. After she is a good distance away, Derrick sternly looks at Jayson.

"I told you to relax," says Derrick.

"I was until Lexia went bonkers. Is she on meds or something? Because she is far from normal," says Jayson.

"Maybe. I haven't seen her take any, though. But you still need to relax."

"I was!"

Derrick looks at the wrecked campsite.

"Who was here?" asks Derrick.

"The Fixers. Me and Lexia took care of them easily, though. Honestly, Mama Bear probably paid cheap for them. They really suck. But, if you don't mind, I'm going to try relaxing again. Maybe sneak into a movie theater or something."

"You go do that. I got some figurines I need to paint."

Jayson grins teasingly. "You still paint toys?"

Derrick's eyes flare with a burst of darkness erupting from him. "They're not toys!"

Jayson holds up his hands defensively. "Alright, my mistake."

Derrick relaxes with a heavy sigh, and then reaches into his wallet. He pulls out a wad of money and puts it in Jayson's hand.

"It's fine," says Derrick. "Here's some cash so you don't go sneaking into the theater. Buy a ticket and enjoy a movie."

"Nice. Thank you!" says Jayson.

"Uh huh. Try to stay out of trouble."

"Say, since you're in a giving mood, can you give me a lift to the theater?"

"Nope. I got figurines to paint."

Derrick gives a heavy pump from his wings, launching him in the air, and leaving Jayson alone in the forest. After Derrick is out of sight, Jayson sighs and hops down to where Mortimer is. The fox has concealed himself with bits of shrub and twigs, but Jayson can see his eyes peeking at him.

"You can relax. The eagle's gone," says Jayson.

Jayson keeps walking, and the bush rustles as Mortimer crawls out, twigs and leaves sticking to his disheveled hair and tail.

"Wait just a minute, Hobo!" calls Mortimer.

Jayson stops and turns to face Mortimer while the fox adjusts his raccoon mask.

"You could have ratted me out, and yet you didn't. Why?" says Mortimer.

Jayson shrugs. "I don't know. I guess I kinda like you. I mean, you're a pain in the ass and shot me, but you make things interesting."

"Ah, I'm glad I can be of service," sneers Mortimer. "But I'm getting paid to kill you, and I will get paid!"

Mortimer draws his pistol and Jayson swiftly yanks out his cosmic weapon, creating the light blue aura. Mortimer shoots at Jayson, but due to the time manipulation, Jayson easily dodges the shot and strikes Mortimer, sending him flying into the creek. As Mortimer is carried away by the current, Jayson continues walking, clutching his side and face twisted to a painful grimace.

****

Claribel's head snaps out of the cold creek water with her Stetson tied around her neck. She gasps for air, her lungs plagued with frozen ice picks poking them from the inside out. She paddles to the shore and claws at the dirt as she crawls her way out.

She flops on her back, chest heaving from her heavy breathing and the mud clings to her clothes, blonde hair, and scales as she stares at the cracked sky. The water weighs her clothes down and it gradually trickles out of the fabric, seeping into the ground and coating her back in mud.

She doesn't know how long she has been laying there until Mortimer staggers next to her and falls on his knees. Then he falls face first to the ground, putting his muzzle next to her cheek and getting a thin amount of her golden blonde hair as a cushion.

"I hate him," grumbles Mortimer.

"I hate her," says Claribel.

"The Hobo is going to the movie theater."

"How can he afford that?"

"The eagle gave him money."

"Oh... Will the Bazooka Bunny be there?"

"Probably."

"Good enough."

The two remain motionless on the ground. Birds chirp and bugs buzz around them, and the water laps at the riverbank. If the situation was different, it would be a tranquil scene that Mortimer would be reluctant to leave.

But alas, they have work to do.

"Ready to go?" asks Mortimer.

"Yeah," replies Claribel.

They remain motionless.

****

Jayson trudges down the cracked sidewalk of Bliss Town, his taped boots grinding against the filth-encrusted pavement. The early afternoon sun beats on his white fur, and various vehicles, corroded and gasping for breath, whip past him while police officers drink and eat inside their police car, with no care of anything around them.

Foot traffic swerves around Jayson, their eyes looking at anything other than him. Yet despite this, Jayson is still humming a merry tune as he walks past a row of various movie posters on a brick wall with faded red and green paint. He only stops humming when he arrives at the entrance of his destination.

Cindy's Cinema.

The theater looks to be stuck in the 1950s, decorated with a neon marquee that wraps around the curved awning and trails up its cylindrical spire, advertising the business. Its once-brilliant paint is flaking off in patches, baring the weathered wood and brick underneath. The neon lights stutter on and off, painting an uncanny luminescence on the fractured pavement in the awning's shade.

Yet despite its decay, Cindy's Cinema clings to life. Its marquee proudly displays the current roster of films, spanning genres from romance, to horror, to action blockbusters. Against all odds, this relic continues to provide entertainment for the community.

Jayson ambles towards the outdoor kiosk, an extension of Cindy's Cinema. It is a retro-futuristic booth, its metallic structure echoing the cinema's art deco styling, with neon lights flickering in sync with the main marquee. Mariana Cross is stationed there, her triangle-checkered vest a stark contrast to the gleaming chrome. Boredom has weighed her face down, and thick black bags are under her dull blue eyes.

Jayson takes a moment to stare at her, and she stares back.

"Don't you work at the Taco King?" asks Jayson.

"Yeah," says Mariana.

"Oh... One ticket to *Cyborg Cop versus Deathbot* please."

"Thirty bucks," says Mariana.

Jayson pays, and Mariana gives him the ticket. Jayson thanks her and gives her one last look before going inside.

The interior matches the exterior with its throwback to the 1950s. Its red velvet curtains and art deco design are bathed in harsh fluorescent light hanging from the ceiling and failing neon lights on the wall. A colossal concession stand dominates the lobby, but it's mostly devoid of life. The employees tucked behind the counter cast skeptical glances at Jayson as he walks towards them with excitement overriding his fatigue. The faded paint on Cindy the Caribou, a white-furred female caribou holding a bucket of popcorn and wearing the awful vest, smiles at Jayson.

"Large popcorn and drink, please. Extra butter on the popcorn and load it up with barbecue powder. Oh, and give me something with a lot of protein," says Jayson.

"We have nacho supreme and hot dogs," says the worker.

Jayson looks at the price on the register, then the prices of the hotdogs and nacho supreme, and finally at the bills in his hand.

"Put on the nacho supreme," says Jayson.

The workers give Jayson his popcorn, nacho supreme, and large drink, and after he fills up his cup, he goes to the ticket master. The ticket master tears his ticket and directs him to go to Theater Room 5. Jayson thanks him and goes to the appropriate theater.

Upon entering Theater Room 5, Jayson finds the temperature to have dropped a bit, and his feet crush old popcorn left behind in the dimly lit room. He climbs the stairs, which have small lights on their steps, and takes a seat at the very back, underneath the projector and near one of the speakers. He sets his weapon between his legs, puts his food and drink in their holders, and stares at the large screen displaying advertisements and trivia, which are signs held up by Cindy the Caribou with various exaggerated expressions, all within the curious to excited emotions.

While Jayson watches the ads and trivia, he pours his nachos into his popcorn, mixing the cheese sauce, the peppers, the ground up meat, sour cream, and lettuce into the bucket of goodness. He munches on his concoction and sips his drink while mentally playing the trivia game. So far, he has a perfect score.

Then, like a bat from the void, Lexia lands next to Jayson. He jumps and his hand snaps onto his cosmic-wood sword while Lexia yanks out a camera and tripod and sets it down next to her. Once that is set up, she reclines on the chair, props her boot-covered feet on the chair in front of her, and aims her pistol at his side, while she fiddles with the camera.

Jayson huffs irritably and releases his grip on his weapon, prompting Lexia to put hers away.

"Lexia, what are you doing?" asks Jayson.

"The movie theater is on my side. I'm making sure you don't ruin it," says Lexia.

"This is neutral territory. By the way, is the gun fake like your chainsaw?"

Lexia holds up her pistol again and turns it so Jayson can see the cartoon cowboy on the side and the orange tip of her barrel.

"Looks fake to me," says Lexia.

"Do you take meds?" asks Jayson.

"What's it to you?"

"Because you're nuts."

"She wants to kill you," says Lexanne, her cold breath brushing against his ear.

Jayson jumps in his seat and curses. The world is darker, and Lexanne is sitting next to him. Her black silhouette a shadow in the dark, her bloody hands grip the arm of the chair while her pale white eyes and white void grin stares at him.

"Get rid of her before she gets rid of you," says Lexanne.

Jayson shakes his head and looks back at the large screen.

"No, she's just being dumb," says Jayson.

"Who's being dumb?" asks Lexia.

"You are."

Lexia gasps. "Am not."

"She tried to kill you in the forest," says Lexanne.

"With a fake chainsaw," retorts Jayson.

"Who are you talking to?" asks Lexia.

"My dead wife," replies Jayson.

Lexia leans over but doesn't see anything. She looks at Jayson.

"You aren't possessed, are you?" she asks.

"No. Of course not. Not even close," replies Jayson sharply.

"So, you are insane! I knew it!"

Jayson bangs his head against his chair. "I just want to watch a movie, alright?"

"Why not a romcom?" suggests Lexanne.

"I hate romcoms," says Jayson.

"I didn't say anything about a romcom," says Lexia. "But this is a nice choice. I love the *Deathbot* and *Cyborg Cop* movies. I can't wait to see them fight."

"Get rid of her. She's ruining our date night," says Lexanne.

"I just want some alone time!" snaps Jayson.

"No can do. I need to record this movie for my mom and make sure you don't wreck this place. Also, Derrick said you needed to relax, so I'm here to make sure you relax," says Lexia.

"Well, you failed. Get lost."

"No."

****

At the alley bordering the movie theater, Claribel and Mortimer approach the side entrance of Cindy's Cinema. Mortimer has a rifle slung on his back and Claribel slips a suppressor on her Thompson rifle. Mortimer uses a lock picking kit to unlock the door with no difficulty.

When the door creaks open, Mortimer goes in while unslinging his weapon. Their first encounter is a lanky rabbit employee counting stock with his "employee of the month" picture nearby on the wall; his name is Leroy.

Leroy's ears perk and his body stiffens when he sees Mortimer and Claribel approaching him with their rifles drawn.

"Hey, you're not supposed to be in here," says Leroy.

Mortimer punches Leroy in the face, and uses nearby tape to gag and hogtie him, and then he puts him in the broom closet. Once that is done, he marches past Claribel.

"Let's go," says Mortimer.

****

Back in Theater Room 5, Jayson stares at the projected images, his eyes heavy, his lips hooked to a frown, and his hands gripping his drink tight, while Lexia and Lexanne talk at the same time, filling both of his ears with despicable noise. Soon the ads and trivia disappear, and a message appears on the silver screen:

ENJOY THE SHOW!

3

****

Mortimer and Claribel walk down the hallway of the cinema, passing brightly lit framed movie posters while employees scatter for cover. The duo spread out, open theater doors, and sniff the air with their noses and tongues.

****

In Theater Room 5, Jayson still tries to ignore Lexia and Lexanne. But the agitation of their overlapping voices brings him to set his drink down and pull his ears down, and squeeze his eyes shut as he breathes heavily.

Then Lexanne's giggle floods into his personal darkness. His eyes snap open, and he looks at her, seeing her grin at him as the countdown continues on the big screen.

"You can feel it, can't you?" says Lexanne.

2

****

Mortimer opens the door to Theater 5 and sniffs the air. His nose picks up the familiar scent of the Hobo Warrior Bunny. He whistles to Claribel, and when she looks at him, he tilts his head to the room while double checking his rifle. Claribel hurries over and they go in with their weapons ready.

****

In Theater Room 5, Jayson and Lexia see light spill into the room and watch two shadows stretch across the floor. Then their eyes bulge and their ears perk when they see Claribel and Mortimer come into view

1

"Showtime," giggles Lexanne.

"SHIT!" yells Lexia.

She leaps up and yanks out her bazooka, and Jayson grabs her arm.

"Lexia, no!" shouts Jayson.

Too late.

Lexia pulls the trigger.

Relaxation- 04

An explosion shakes Theater Room 5 as the blast rips through its wall, flinging fire and debris into the neighboring theater while dust rolls through the air. Jayson and Lexia duck for cover as Claribel and Mortimer shoot back at them, their bullets tearing through the half-wall lining the stairs. An alarm rings and the lights flash on while movie trailers play on the big screen.

Lexia gets up again and shoots another rocket at Claribel. The rattlesnake dives into the chairs, and the rocket streaks past her and blows apart the floor, tossing shattered floor bits all around.

Smoke and dust linger in the air, and Mortimer runs up the stairs and shoots Lexia while she reloads her bazooka. The bullets hit her armor, dropping her to the ground, and leave her cursing and scrambling for shelter in the chairs while Mortimer continues shooting.

The bullets tear apart the chairs, and Jayson leaps from his cover and hops on top of the railings separating the rows of chairs. He yells and takes a flying kick to Mortimer, hitting him in the shoulder.

Mortimer hits the half-wall, Jayson lands awkwardly, and both of them roll down the stairs in a jumbled mess of limbs. When they stop rolling, Mortimer kicks Jayson away, and scrambles for his rifle.

As this happens, Jayson draws his wooden sword. After Mortimer grabs his rifle, he turns to shoot Jayson but is whacked with the cosmic weapon.

The strike breaks him through the stairway barrier and smacks him against the wall on the other side, where he tumbles down and lands flat on the floor with rubble around him, leaving his body imprint at the point of impact.

Suddenly, two bullets rip into Jayson's arm and shoulder, dropping him and forcing him to crawl to safety while more bullets zip towards him, breaking more chairs.

Claribel stays low as she goes up the stairs, keeping her sights trained on Jayson and firing off another round when she sees movement behind the chairs.

Meanwhile, Lexia pokes her head out, just to duck down when Claribel shoots at her, punching a hole in the chair next to her head. Lexia pulls a grenade from thin air, yanks the pin out with her teeth, and chucks the explosive at Claribel.

The grenade bounces down the stairs, and Claribel ducks into a chair-row and shields herself as the device explodes. She winces as heat washes over her and shrapnel punctures the chairs and wall.

With smoke lingering in the air, Lexia gets on her knees, pulls out a mini gun on a tripod, and she screams maniacally as she unloads in Claribel's direction.

As Lexia screams and cackles, Jayson peeks up and his ears droop from the sight of the chairs and floor dissolving from the stream of bullets ripping through them. His ears are ringing, his heart races, and his eyes flick between Lexia and the location she is destroying.

Jayson sees Claribel slithering through the chaos for a brief moment, and a second after she disappears from sight, a muzzle flash briefly illuminates her spot. A large lamp snaps loose from the ceiling and hits Lexia on the head, knocking her to the floor with her eyes rolling and head bleeding.

"Lexia!" cries Jayson.

Jayson gets up, clutching his arm, and he runs towards Lexia's position, just to be tackled by Mortimer. The impact pushes Jayson against the folded chairs, and he kicks Mortimer away, sending him tumbling off the railing and falling onto the next row of chairs.

Jayson's old wounds throb and his fresh ones burn, and he grits his teeth while trying to get to Lexia again, but Mortimer grabs him by his collar, swings him around, and slams him to the floor. Jayson's vision is knocked out of focus, but he registers enough to hold his arm up to stop Mortimer from biting his neck.

The fox growls and twists his head while his claws tear at Jayson's shoulders.

Jayson screams and curses as Mortimer's motions slam him against the chair bottoms and railing.

Blood pours down his arm and shoulders, and Jayson uses his smaller claws to slash Mortimer's face, opening his burnt flesh around the eye.

Mortimer yelps and releases Jayson long enough for Jayson to kick him off, and then knocks him on his back and pummels him in the face a few times before Mortimer retaliates.

It is a blur of motion and a vicious mixture of snarls and yells that leads to the two rolling around and bouncing down the stairs, each with a flash of pain and disorientation.

When they stop rolling, Jayson draws his cosmic weapon and holds it against Mortimer as he goes for another bite. The fox's teeth do nothing to the wood as he bites down on it, and Jayson grinds his teeth, arms burning, blood hot and flowing freely from his wounds.

He kicks Mortimer off and rolls to his knees, panting and dripping sweat and blood.

A rocket streaks by a moment later, blowing up a section of the chairs. While burning chair bits rain down, Mortimer charges Jayson, and Jayson tries to activate the aura, but it fizzles out and leaves his already weakened body feeling worse with trembles, a heavy heart, and shallow breaths.

Jayson's mouth falls open as he gasps for air, and his legs get weak, causing him to stumble. This gives Mortimer enough time to grab Jayson and throw him against the stair's half-wall.

His weapon falls from his grip and Mortimer kicks it down the stairs before going for fast slashes, which Jayson blocks with some difficulty.

Jayson sweats as ragged breath burst through his gritted teeth and nose. His arm becomes red with blood as the cuts grow, and when Mortimer goes for a slash aimed at his head, Jayson ducks and punches him in the kidney.

Mortimer staggers, and Jayson pivots around him, kicks out his leg, and slams his head into the wall.

Mortimer drops down, clutching his bleeding face and cursing up a storm, while Jayson jumps towards his cosmic-wood sword, plucks it up, and tries again with the aura. It stays this time, but the discomfort is still there.

His world darkens as he focuses on Mortimer. His breathing gets heavier and more labored, his heart pounds erratically, and his limbs tremble as he rushes up the stairs.

Time crawls as Mortimer stands and turns, and his eyes widen as Jayson propels towards him, hands tight, eyes wide, and mouth open from his scream. Jayson hits Mortimer in the gut, sending the fox flying.

After he hits him, the aura disappears, and Jayson drops to his knees, using his weapon for support as he coughs and heaves. His limbs quiver, every wound - old and new - throbs and burns, and Lexanne chuckles nearby, her body a silhouette in the growing smoke in Theater Room 5.

As Jayson tries to regain his breathing, his hand rubs his heart and his eyes drift to Lexia, whose white and brown fur and white hair are a mess of blood. The harlequin-hare is launching another rocket at Claribel, and the snake dives over the edge of the stairs but is still pushed into the wall by the resulting explosion.

Burning debris rains down, and Claribel bolts towards the exit while Lexia climbs on top of the wall as she reloads. She shoots another rocket at Claribel when the snake reaches the door.

The resulting explosion sends Claribel flying out into the hallway with debris following close behind. She hits the nearby wall and goes still.

Inside Theater Room 5, Jayson pushes himself up while sheathing his weapon. His legs are quivering, and his fingers are weak, and he takes a couple of steps towards Lexia before falling over and grabbing a destroyed chair for support.

Lexia immediately rushes to him, grabs his bloody hand, and tugs him down the wrecked stairs, towards the emergency exit. Lexia pushes the door open with her shoulder and drags Jayson down the alley towards a light-brown, four-door car that is equipped with thick windows, light-brown armor plating, antennas of various sizes, and a small satellite dish on the roof.

Police sirens rapidly approach. Lexia nearly throws Jayson against her car's passenger door while she slides over the hood to get to the driver's side.

"Get in! The door doesn't lock!" says Lexia while throwing her bazooka in the back seat.

Jayson gets in the passenger seat and places his weapon between his legs. Lexia jumps in the driver's seat, revs the engine, and the tires squeal against the old asphalt as they speed away, leaving Cindy's Cinema to suffer from their fight with the Fixers.

Inside the spacious interior of the car, Jayson and Lexia stare ahead while police cars and fire trucks zoom by them. They drive in silence, bleeding all over the dark brown seats while a *Block World* cube dangles from the rear view mirror. They drive for another couple of minutes, and when they reach a red light, they stare ahead in silence for another few seconds.

But that silence is broken when Jayson speaks. "'The movie theater is on my side,' you said. 'I don't want you to ruin it,' you said."

Lexia frowns and tightens her grip on the steering wheel.

"'***I don't want you to ruin it,' you said,***" repeats Jayson.

"I know," says Lexia heavily.

"You did more damage to the theater than I ever could."

"Yeah? Well... You're bleeding all over my seat."

"So are you!"

"I'm allowed to bleed on my seats! Unlike you! You're not allowed to bleed. Especially on my seats!"

The light turns green, Lexia drives on, and Jayson scoffs and opens the glove compartment box, finding a big box of Band-Aids.

"Oh, sorry! I didn't mean to get shot again! I was the one trying to relax and you were the nut who chased me with a chainsaw and then launched rockets everywhere!" says Jayson as he removes his torn jacket, exposing his shredded blue shirt, now stained in fresh blood.

Lexia sharply veers the car back and forth, making Jayson hit his head on the window and drop the Band-Aids.

"Ow! Damn it, Lexia! You're a psycho!" says Jayson as he picks up the Bands-Aids from the floor.

"You were literally talking to your dead wife," says Lexia.

Jayson starts applying Band-Aids to his collection of injuries. "Because I'm lonely and actually care about people! It's a loss that I will never get over. You wouldn't understand because you're a heartless lunatic with some serious issues!"

"Hey, I care about people."

"Oh really? Like who?"

"Not you. You're not on my list. My mom is on my list, and oh my God, I left my camera and mini gun at the theater." Lexia bangs her fist on the steering wheel. "Dang it!"

Jayson snorts a laugh. "Well, you're getting arrested now."

"Please, they never arrest anybody here. If they did, I wouldn't have to kill criminals with rockets."

"Rockets that you shoot really close to me. Honestly, I'm surprised your antics haven't killed me yet."

"Same. Maybe one day I'll get lucky."

Jayson glares at Lexia.

"Do you want a taco? I want a taco," says Lexia.

Jayson sighs heavily. "You know what? Yeah, I can use a burrito."

"Great!"

Lexia takes a sharp turn and the tires squeal as she zooms towards the Taco King drive-thru. Then she slams on the brakes when they are near the speaker box. Black streaks stain the asphalt and the vehicle jerks to a stop with Lexia's window directly bordering the speaker.

"Welcome to Taco King. What do you want?" says Mariana Cross, her voice crackly and barely understandable through the speaker.

"I want a taco," says Lexia.

****

Back at the safehouse, Ramsey, Rolland, Shae, Dacre, and Cyrus are playing One-O in the living room. Everyone is sitting on the floor around the coffee table, and with them are various snacks and drinks, and a large plastic sheet is covering the carpet. Said sheet is already messy with spilled dipping sauce and drinks, and the colorful cards of One-O lay in a sloppy pile in the middle of the table.

"Okay, after this, I really need to get back to work," says Ramsey.

"Yeah, yeah, just play the card," says Rolland.

Ramsey puts down a card. "One-O."

Rolland puts down a card. "One-O."

Shae puts down a card. "One-O."

Dacre puts down a card. "One-O."

Cyrus puts down a card. "Wild. Red. One-O."

Ramsey puts down his last card, a red reverse. "I win. I need to get back to work. Narcotics won't make themselves."

Suddenly, the front door bangs open, prompting Rolland's group to snap out their pistols and aim at the noise while Ramsey dives for cover behind the couch. A moment of silence passes, and Rolland's group's eyes widen, and they lower their weapons, and Ramsey peeks his head out from cover. Mortimer and Claribel stumble in, bloodied, bruised, covered in soot, their clothes torn, and their bodies burning from the sheer rage.

"Holy shit... What happened to you two?" asks Rolland.

Mortimer takes a deep breath. "We need... Tacos."

****

Back inside Lexia's car, Lexia is eating a taco, and Jayson is eating a burrito. They are quiet while Lexia drives with one hand. Both of them are covered in an abundance of Band-Aids, and behind Jayson is Lexanne; her white grin nearly severing her jaw from the rest of her face.

"She doesn't care about you," says Lexanne.

Jayson looks at Lexanne through the mirror.

"But I care about you. We're forever and ever, remember?" says Lexanne.

Jayson blinks and Lexanne is gone, and he looks at Lexia.

"So, Lexia...?" says Jayson.

"Yeah?" says Lexia.

"About what you said."

"One-hundred-percent true. I don't care about you. At all. Not even close. I care about my mom, though."

"What about Derrick?"

Lexia shrugs. "Eh... Kinda. He knew my dad. They were friends in the police force, so I kinda like him. But you're encroaching on my turf, and I'm only sort of tolerating you because Derrick wants me to."

"I see... Stop the car."

Lexia slows the car to a stop at the edge of the forest, and Jayson gets out, politely closes the door, hobbles to Lexia's side, and winces when he leans against the window. Lexia rolls down her window, and he props his elbows on the rim.

"Thanks for the ride, and the burrito, but I'm going to go home now," says Jayson.

"Do you seriously live in the forest?" asks Lexia.

"Where else am I going to live? I'm a hobo, remember." Before Lexia can respond, he taps the window rim and walks away while waving farewell with his back to Lexia. "Have a good one. I'll see you sometime in the future."

Lexia watches him quietly, and Jayson hops down a ravine and resumes hobbling with one hand in his coat pocket and the other clutching his side, keeping his eyes locked ahead and his jaw set. He can feel Lexia watching him, and he picks up his pace. It's only when he passes through the tree line does he hear her vehicle rev and drive away. When that happens, he takes a deep breath, dips his head, and kicks a random rock as he walks through the forest alone.

Inside the car, Lexia stares ahead, her hands tight on the steering wheel, her wrapper tossed aside, and her other hand on the stick shift. Her grip tightens and her lips quiver, and her breathing becomes heavier as her eyes become wet. But she holds it in and keeps driving in silence.

****

Back at the safehouse, Mortimer and Claribel are laying on Mortimer's bed. Claribel is snuggled on top of him, her tail wrapped around his torso and his arm over her shoulder. Mortimer stares at the ceiling, and Claribel stares at the wall. Both haven't said a word, but their hold on each other is sturdy and protective. Minutes tick by before Ramsey pokes his head in.

RELAXATION- 04

"Hey, we just ordered a delivery from Taco King. We got a big meal coming our way," says Ramsey.

Mortimer gives Ramsey a thumb-up. "Thanks."

Ramsey leaves, and Mortimer sighs heavily and rubs Claribel's shoulder, and she rubs her head underneath his chin and closes her eyes. Then the radio in Mortimer's room crackles and a heavy voice breaches the silence.

"Static Boy, are you there?"

Mortimer and Claribel's eyes snap open, and their heads turn to the radio.

"You better be there," says the voice.

Mortimer gently removes Claribel from his body and goes to the radio. His hands tremble and his throat tightens as he reluctantly reaches for it.

"You have ten seconds to pick up. Starting now," says the voice.

Mortimer snatches the radio and leans against the wall, putting on a cool smile.

"Hey, Thaddeus, is that you?" says Mortimer.

"You know it's me," says Thaddeus. *"What's the update on the Hobo Warrior Bunny and Bazooka Bunny?"*

"Oh them? Me and Claribel are handling it."

"So, they're not dead yet."

"Not yet. But we're getting there."

"Am I going to have to come down there?"

"NO!" Mortimer clears his throat and wipes his face. "I mean, no, it's fine. We're fine. We got this under control."

"Mama Bear thinks otherwise."

"Is Mama Bear with you now?"

"What do you think?"

Mortimer's eyes are wide and staring ahead, and Claribel holds the pillow against her body as she stares at Mortimer with worry suffocating her.

"Get it done. Or I'm coming down there. And if I have to come down there, then I'll be dealing with you and your snake personally," says Thaddeus.

The radio clicks off, and Mortimer hangs up the radio head and looks at Claribel. She stares at him with watery eyes, and he offers a comforting smile.

"We'll be fine... I promise," says Mortimer.

****

The late afternoon sun shines high in the cracked sky. Birds chirp, leaves rustle, and flowers sway in the wind. Jayson Hopper limps through a crumbled brick wall, passing a rusted gate ensnared by vines and trees. He keeps walking, stepping on broken cobblestone and passing rotten wooden and brick structures that are collapsing on themselves. His old and new wounds throb, and his eyes and breathing are heavy.

He goes to a bus stop with an advertisement faded away and its glass shattered. He draws his cosmic-wood sword, sits on the bench with the weapon between his legs, and he stares ahead at a statue of a family of six eating a picnic, surrounded by green trees and red roses, and the sign beneath them says: *"Wonderful Abode Is Here for Your Wonderful World."*

The details of the statue have faded from time and weather, and large portions have crumbed away, exposing the rusting metal skeletons beneath the concrete. Someone also spray-painted blue on the food and numerous butterflies on the family, and scribbled over the sign is, *"Reel Sight is Better than Real Sight."*

Jayson takes a deep breath, rubs his slow and heavy heart, and closes his eyes. They remain closed for several seconds, and after he opens them, he sees Lexanne standing in front of him. Her solid black, shadowy figure towers over Jayson. Her torn fabric and hair float as if in water, and her pure white eyes stare at Jayson while blood drips from the red lines trailing the length of her forearms.

"Are you winning, Jayson?" teases Lexanne.

"What do you care?" says Jayson.

Lexanne holds out her hands. "Let me take you out of here. Come see with me."

Jayson shakes his head and winces as he stands up, using his weapon for support.

"I can't," says Jayson.

"You can," says Lexanne.

"I don't want to."

"Where's the harm in seeing again? You miss it, don't you? The colors, the bliss. The sweet, sweet bliss. All your troubles gone for that one moment."

Jayson walks away, shaking his head and using his weapon as a cane.

"I'm not dealing with this, right now," says Jayson.

Lexanne giggles and floats next to Jayson, her cold hands rubbing his shoulders and her mouth next to his ear.

"Running again?" taunts Lexanne.

"I'm not running," says Jayson.

"*Righhht...* You're not running. You never run. Or are you sad because I was right about Lexia?"

"I'm definitely not sad about that. She's tried to kill me multiple times, so it's obvious she doesn't like me."

Lexanne shifts in front of Jayson and grabs his shoulder and hand, her grin taking up his entire field of vision.

"Don't be sad, Jayson. I'm here. I've always been here, and I'll always be here. And when your time comes, I'll be waiting for you, and we'll see together for all eternity. Won't that be great?"

Jayson glares at Lexanne with heavy wet eyes, and she giggles and brushes Jayson's cheek.

"I'll leave you be for now. You had a long day, and now you need to relax. I'll be seeing you in the future," says Lexanne.

Lexanne vanishes after that, and a coldness envelopes Jayson as all noise fades in the abandoned town. Jayson exhales a shaky breath, his back thudding against a tree growing through what was once a parking lot.

With a heavy heart, he sinks to the broken asphalt, pressing his forehead into clenched fists. The words of Lexanne linger in his mind. The air becomes thick, and Jayson's breaths tremble as he realizes that the torment will continue indefinitely. Perhaps one day he'll find peace, but for now, that is out of his reach.

"What a lousy world," says Jayson.

IV

Bliss Town Reservoir

Derrick convinces Jayson and Lexia to go to the Bliss Town Reservoir. Coincidentally, Mortimer also convinces Claribel to go to the reservoir. What ensues is a moment of peace between the two factions.

Bliss Town Reservoir- 01

Distant thumps echo in the void from the shifting cracks in the sky, creating ripples of light blue that travel through the dark water. The clock-shaped, bright blue cracks in the sky spread as far as the eye can see. The anomaly provides some light, but it is not enough for Jayson to see far.

Jayson stands in the ankle-deep water. Wet warmth seeps through his boots and socks while the cracks above him shift as hour, minute, and seconds hands, each going at appropriate speeds. In front of Jayson is a door with bloody water gurgling past it, and red light seeping through its borders.

Jayson tries to back up, but bony hands grab his ankles, holding him firmly in place. The door cracks open. Jayson's heart races as red light pours over him, and in the center of the room beyond the door is a bathtub, overflowing with crimson-tainted water.

A single white hand hangs limply over the edge. It sits like this for a few seconds before it twists, bones cracking and elbow popping. The white shifts to black, the hand points at Jayson, and it beckons him forward.

"Come see with me," says Lexanne.

(((***)))

Jayson's eyes snap open, putting a damp ceiling in his vision. The wood of the chilly, desolate burrow is rotting and snapping, but support pillars manage to keep the roof up. Nearby is a Ouija board, decorated with butterflies, and an empty can of beans lays next to a pile of burnt wood and a shirt ruined from the fight with Mortimer. They are contained by a ring of old bricks.

Jayson rolls on his hands and knees, shifting a tattered and discolored blanket off him, exposing a scattered network of fading bruises and scars. He coughs and hacks, his fingers digging into the dirt that used to be a floor, while his other hand rubs his heart. He pushes himself on his knees and rubs his eyes.

Blinking the haze out of his vision, he crawls to a crate and digs out some clothes, which all have various shades of blue. The only things the same are his jacket and scarf, which is still stained with old blood, and his jacket has been crudely stitched back together.

Jayson slips on his jacket, adjusts his scarf, and puts his boots on. After that, he fastens his makeshift sheath to his belt and checks to make sure his cosmic-wood sword is working.

He swiftly yanks it out, and with fluid motions gives it a few swings, watching with a satisfied smile as the aura appears and fades seconds later. There is still some discomfort in his chest, but not nearly as bad as it was the day prior, telling him that a good rest is what he needed.

After sliding his weapon back in its sheath, he takes a deep breath to steady his heart, and resumes practicing his quick draw.

He snaps his cosmic weapon out, swings it a few times, and slides it back in. He takes another deep breath and repeats. This process continues with no break for an unknown amount of time, and it leaves Jayson panting, but satisfied and glad that his wounds are not giving him crippling pain.

After Jayson finishes practicing, he moves aside a door made out of pallets, revealing the forest before him and many abandoned bunny burrows with their mailboxes and doors rotting away. Evergreen trees and red roses grow rampantly throughout the abandoned community, and graffiti on the houses have faded from the weather and plants growing along the structures. The morning light shines past the thinning orange and red canopy of leaves, and Jayson grabs a large burlap bag and heads out, forcing himself to whistle a cheerful tune.

****

The grandfather clock lying on the floor ticks unevenly, its noises barely making a thump in the desolate treehouse. Early morning light pours through the glass patio door, and Derrick sits at his dining room table, a cup of coffee on one side, and various mugs of paint-tainted water on the other.

Plastic figurines ranging from soldiers to vehicles, and small paint containers of various colors, clutter the table, which is protected by multiple sheets of wax paper. The completed figures are in a separate corner, steadily drying, while the unpainted gray ones are lined up in uniform, waiting to get their colors.

Currently, Derrick is painting a boxy tank with two large cannons and four machine gun turrets being operated by poorly protected soldiers. The base blue color is already covering the bulky figure, but now he is using a magnifying glass set up on a small pedestal to help him paint the first soldier, using a fine-tipped brush for the details.

The soldier gradually gets color, and when the soldier is complete, Derrick puts down his brush and runs his talons through his plumage. He remains motionless with his hands covering his eyes for a few seconds before he clamps them in front of his beak.

The ticking continues, and his eyes drift to the locked door. He exhales heavily and returns his attention to the figurines. While he wants to continue painting, his hands refuse to move.

Nausea seeps in and he pushes himself away from the table without leaving his chair.

The ticking continues and Derrick looks at one of his painted figurines. It is one of a dozen futuristic amphibious assault crafts with little soldiers inside it (the other eleven still need painting). He added battle damage to the vehicle and soldiers' armor, giving them burns, bullet dings, and scratches, as well as a last-minute addition of a female anthro-shark painted on the side, winking, and holding a harpoon gun. The addition also has the damages put on to match the rest of the ship.

His eyes drift away from the figurines and look at a wall with rectangular patches discoloring portions of the wall. All that remains is a picture of a stretch of clean blue waters and lush green trees, all under the soft white clouds hiding the cracked blue sky.

"You're taking the pictures, too!" yelled Derrick.

"Yes, it's better for them to not remember you, and God willing, you forget what they look like!" yelled a female, her voice broken with tears.

Derrick grabs the lone picture off the wall and inspects it. His heavy eyes reflect back to him, and his hands tremble as he carefully returns the picture and goes to his gun safe.

He opens it without putting in a combination, pulls out his rifle, and sits on his chair, facing the picture of the reservoir.

He closes his eyes, rests his head against the barrel and waits.

Bliss Town Reservoir- 02

The morning sun warms Jayson's back as his filthy fingers rummage through the refuse collected in the public garbage can. Wrappers and old paper crinkle from his shifting, releasing clouds of rotten stench that no longer faze him. Soda cans clink and clank and bottle caps click against each other as he tosses them into the burlap sack laying open at his feet. His fingers move with surgical precision and his eyes scan the trash for more signs of precious scrap metal.

****

Across the street, Lexia sits behind a bench. Her homemade armor coupled with her bazooka, and mismatched fur serve as useless camouflage. Passing pedestrians give quick glances at her but keep on moving without saying a word or tugging their child away before they can pester the harlequin-hare.

With a notebook on one knee, and satellite audio observation device in her hand, she madly scribbles her notes, risking only a second at a time to make sure her letters are on the pink lines. For today she is not Lexia Hartwick the Bazooka Bunny. Today she is Dr. Lexia Hartwick, scientist extraordinaire, on a mission to collect data on Jaysonious Hopperificicus.

****

Jayson keeps to his task. He sees Lexia spying on him from across the street but ignores her. He's on a mission and she is clearly bored. So far, no trouble has come from the Fixers or any of Mama Bear's weaker associates, so they have nothing better to do. Besides, she's still on her side, so he can't do much to her.

Jayson clutches his bag tightly and walks down the sidewalk to the next public garbage can. He pulls off its lid and starts sifting through it, the crinkles, clatters, and clangs of his rummaging serving as a tuneless symphony to the hellish city around them. Bottle caps, soda cans, and some spoons are tossed in his sack, and he glances up to see Lexia hiding by a tree, aiming her little satellite at him.

Jayson resumes digging. But he pauses for a moment, and then grins as he pulls out a half-eaten black bean burrito.

"Nice," hisses Jayson to himself. He looks at Lexia and takes a massive bite from it and shudders at the delicious taste of cold beans, old zesty ranch, soggy lettuce, and dissolved flour tortilla.

He can see Lexia's eye twitching, and he grins with his lips sealed tight to hold the food as he sets his new meal down on some old paper. After that, he continues plucking caps, cans, tabs, paperclips, and other bits of small metal from the trash.

****

Across the street, Lexia lips have curled to a disgusted sneer, and she scribbles in her notes:

Dr. Lexia Hartwick log #12345.

Jaysonious Hopperificicus is still digging through the trash. He saw through my camouflage and is now mocking me by being disgusting. This is probably why he's not acting like a total weirdo this time. Unlike last time at the movie theater when he talked to his dead wife. (Note to self, ask about that when given the opportunity and don't be weird about it)

Jaysonious Hopperificicus is still digging through the trash. He likes burritos. Which is gross. Everyone knows a taco is better. Now if he'd talk to his dead wife again so I can get a transcript that'd be great.

Lexia stops writing and rubs the sweat from her face. Then casts an annoyed glare at the cloudless, cracked afternoon sky and quickly scribbles another note in her book.

Note to self: Buy an umbrella hat.

****

The sun keeps rising, warped beyond the cracks, casting its relentless heat across the littered pavement. And across the street, Jayson's bag steadily gains a satisfactory weight that promises food from the value menu. He even snags a few crinkled coupons that have a few days left on them.

One is for Samantha's Spa. Another for Arty's Arcade. And then there's a few for Taco King and the Sam and Mann Supermarket. All stained with old mustard.

Jayson smirks, folds the spa coupon into a paper airplane, and throws it across the street. The air currents carry the small object over the road, and the paper craft does a twirl, a dive, and lands in Lexia's hair.

Jayson snickers and goes back to his rummaging while Lexia plucks the nasty coupon out of her hair.

"Dang it, Jayson! I just washed my hair!" shouts Lexia, her voice echoing across the street.

Jayson gives a thumb-up without looking at her and continues his scavenging.

****

Lexia unfolds the paper airplane Jayson threw at her and studies the filthy coupon page.

Are you a grumpy bunny? Do people say you stink? Has stress made you hideous? Come on down to Samantha's Spa for a Super-Duper Deep Cleaning Mega Pampering Session!

Below that message is the discount. Two percent off the session, which includes manicure, pedicure, full body massages, mud bath, steam room, and deep cleaning.

Lexia scoffs. "Very funny, Jayson."

She looks across the street, sees he isn't looking at her, so she quickly stuffs it in her knife sheath before continuing her observation. As she watches Jayson, a shadow looms over her.

Lexia stiffens and slowly turns her head to see Derrick staring down at her, holding a large cooler and beach umbrella with his rifle on his back, and wearing a light-colored flowery shirt. In his beak is a lit cigarette.

"What are you doing, Lexia?" says Derrick, his voice tinged with disapproval.

"Research," says Lexia. She flicks her eyes up and down Derrick's outfit and sneers when she sees sandals and socks on his feet. "What are you wearing, and why are you wearing it?"

"You look like you're spying."

"It's not spying. It's research."

Derrick looks over her shoulder, his large eyes scanning her scribbles.

"You trying to figure out what to get Jayson for Christmas?" says Derrick.

"No!" snaps Lexia, her hand covering the page. "Jayson claims he talks to his dead wife, so I was trying to see how often he does that."

She looks back across the street, but sees that Jayson is gone, and she huffs and slaps her notebook against her thigh.

"Great. He wandered off. Thanks a lot, Derrick," says Lexia.

"No problem," says Derrick. "Meet me at the Bliss Town Reservoir."

"Why?"

"We're taking a break today. Swimming, hotdogs, living life. Good stuff to make good memories since you and Jayson have had a rough few days."

"Breaks are for the weak," claims Lexia.

A red tint takes over Derrick's pupils as he narrows his eyes, and the area darkens around them. Lexia smiles nervously and stands up, holding her notebook and audio spy equipment close to her.

"I mean, I'll get my bathing suit," says Lexia.

The area brightens, and a small smile tugs at the edge of Derrick's beak.

"Good. I'll get Jayson," says Derrick.

He flies away, and Lexia deflates with a heavy sigh and trudges down the sidewalk.

"Man, I'm surrounded by weirdos," says Lexia.

BLISS TOWN RESERVOIR- 02

****

Jayson walks into an alley, bag slung over his shoulder and a wordless hum vibrating in his throat. He passes graffiti of a winged DNA strand over a graveyard, art of broadly smiling people with butterflies coming out of their eyes, and bullet holes on the walls of old buildings.

He approaches a dumpster with phone numbers and doodles marking its peeling green paint. He flips the lid open, props it up with an old piece of wood from a broken pallet, and climbs in.

After a few minutes of rummaging and tossing out bent cans of various origins, bottle caps, and other small metal pieces, he hops out, just to come nearly face to face with Derrick. The sudden appearance makes him jump back with a short yell and clutch his wooden weapon's hilt, but he quickly relaxes and takes a deep breath to steady his racing heart.

"Jeeze Derrick, are you trying to give me a heart attack?" Jayson sees the supplies in Derrick's hands, and the colorful flower shirt he's wearing. Then his eyes lock onto the socks and sandals. "What's with the... stuff?"

"Reservoir day," says Derrick.

"Oh, nice. Well, have fun with that."

"You're coming."

Jayson kneels down and collects his findings. "Can't. I have scrap metal to sell."

"The scrap metal place doesn't close until nine pm."

"I also hate sand."

"Since when?"

"Always."

"You sleep in dirt."

"Which is different from sand."

"Jayson, you need to relax. You and Lexia have had a rough streak. So, if I don't see you at the reservoir to have fun and unwind by the time I am finished cooking these hotdogs, I will find you, I will drag you to the reservoir, and I will dunk you. Are we clear?"

Jayson stares at Derrick with wide eyes and tight lips, and Derrick stares back with narrow red eyes and a dark aura around him. Several seconds pass, and Jayson flips a thumb-up.

"I'll be there," says Jayson.

The world brightens and Derrick smiles.

"Good," says Derrick.

Then he flies away, and Jayson exhales and runs his gunky fingers through his filthy hair.

"Well... That just happened," says Jayson.

****

Computer keys and mouse buttons click loudly in Claribel's room. Her red reptilian eyes focus intently on the screen as her mouse avatar, Ms. Fritz Bee, dressed in a safari outfit, hops along the blocky landscape, and furiously mines the gold-colored bricks. The clanging and breaking stone floods her ears from through her headset.

She is focused.

She is lost in her world.

She is yanked off her chair, tugging the headphones out of the jack, and goes airborne. She yells as she lands on her back on the bed and Mortimer jumps on top of her, trapping her between his arms and legs with a wide, sharp-toothed grin on his burnt face. Claribel's shocked expression reflects back on her from Mortimer's wide, sparkly eyes, his muzzle a mere inch from her nose. His hands and feet dig into the mattress, locking him in place, while Claribel has her hands pressed against his chest.

"Mortimer are you trying to get bit!" says Claribel.

"Let's go to the reservoir, Claribel!" says Mortimer, his large fox tail wagging and completely unconcerned about the threat of death.

"What?"

Mortimer sits on Claribel's lap and takes out a flyer advertising a crystal-clear body of water with lush trees and happy people cooking on grills and playing in the water, all under a bright, sunny, cracked sky.

"The Bliss Town Reservoir has everything we need to relax. Water, food court, shade, free grills!" Mortimer crunches the flyer in his hand as he sighs whimsically. "I can finally feel the soft sand on my feet again."

Claribel props herself up on her elbows. "Mortimer, are you trying to calm yourself down after talking to Thaddeus?"

"Psh. Of course not. He doesn't scare me at all. But!" Mortimer grabs Claribel's shoulders and goes muzzle to nose with her again. "We do need to unwind after the nightmare we've been through trying to get rid of the Hobo Warrior Bunny and Bazooka Bunny."

"But my game..." says Claribel, her eyes shifting to her monitor just in time to see Ms. Fritz Bee get swarmed by spiders and die. Her avatar disappears in a puff of colorful smoke, leaving a tombstone behind. Claribel frowns at that. "And now she's dead."

"Relax, your character revives."

"Respawns. And she doesn't this time because it was a perma-death challenge," says Claribel sourly.

"Okay, think of it like this. Your avatar can *respawn* and *relive* save points, but people in real life do not. When the moment is gone, it is gone forever. So, come on and live this moment with me. Please!" says Mortimer.

Claribel looks at Mortimer again, and his smile does a poor job of hiding the desperation and he swishes his tail against hers. Her frown holds. His smile strains. Seconds tick by, and she groans and flops on her back.

"Fine," says Claribel.

"Yes!" Mortimer kisses Claribel's lips and scampers away. "Funness here we come!"

The door slams shut, and Claribel stays on her back, blushing in silence.

Bliss Town Reservoir- 03

Jayson's long, jagged shadow stretches across the cracked pavement as he approaches the Bliss Town Reservoir. The bag over his shoulder clinks with the sound of scavenged metal. Soda cans, beer cans, empty food cans, bottle caps, and other bits of treasure smack against each other, and it is all music to Jayson's ears.

He stops by the toll booth but sees the operator staring off into space with a goofy smile and dilated eyes. His fingers tap on the counter as if it is a piano and sweat pours down his face.

Jayson frowns, reaches through the window to open the door. Then he slips into the booth, activates a large fan in the corner, and turns the operator to it. His fingers are still moving as if he is playing a piano, and he giggles and rolls his head.

"Thanks, butterflies," says the operator.

"No problem," says Jayson, patting his shoulder.

Jayson locks the booth door before exiting, and he resumes walking across the cracked asphalt and its faded parking lines. Gradually the tree line gets closer and with it the gentle waves and happy chatter of people enjoying the afternoon.

Jayson's smile grows, and he walks down some discolored concrete steps, passing weeds engulfing grass and looming trees suffering from malnutrition.

When Jayson passes through the trees and finally reaches the reservoir, the expected clean waters and welcoming nature is met with the harsh reality that is Bliss Town.

The reservoir is a sad sight, a once-vibrant body of water now choked with algae and the detritus of urban decay. Plastic bags cling to partially submerged rocks, while rusted shopping carts lay scattered around the area or stacked on top of each other as a mockery of modern art. Graffiti desecrates the concrete banks with colorful but malignant art. And distant boats and jet skis sputter as careless people chuck trash in the water.

Off to the side of this dismal scene, using a tree with a spotty canopy as shade, stands Derrick. His massive eagle frame hunched over a battered public grill while a splintering picnic table is occupied by paper plates, chips, and potato salad. The small grill is lit up and sending tendrils of black smoke to the sky. He is meticulously arranging the charcoal with his clippers while the fire darkens and bubbles the hotdog skins.

"I thought I was going to have to drag you over here," says Derrick without looking up from his work.

"I almost wanted to see you try," admits Jayson, dropping his bag with a metallic thud. He scans the decaying recreational spot and shakes his head with his hands on his hips. "This place... it's a dump. So much property value wasted."

"Yup. But it's our dump for today," says Derrick, a wry twist to his beak. He finally glances at Jayson, taking in the white fur stained by life on the streets, the blue scarf dulled by blood, grime and sweat, and his brown hair tangled. "You look like hell."

"Getting, shot, bit, and tossed around does that to people," says Jayson, leaning on his weapon like a crutch. "But you're right. A little relaxation will get me feeling better."

Derrick releases a puff of smoke. "That's why I told you and Lexia to get over here. You have been running on fumes and I've dealt with a few Fixers before, but them new ones are something else. Both of you need to relax a bit before you snap or get killed from exhaustion."

"Lexia actually agreed to this?" Jayson's ears perked up with a mix of suspicion and curiosity.

"Yep. I had to twist her arm a bit. She's as stubborn as you are."

"Great," groans Jayson.

"Don't you start with that," says Derrick sternly. "Now sit your furry ass down and take a load off."

Jayson releases a short, barking laugh, devoid of real humor, as he approaches the table with his bag in hand.

"Alright, boss," says Jayson. He drops the bag at his feet as he sits at the picnic table. "But if I find a fish head in my hotdog bun, we're going to have words."

"Relax, I won't be doing that today," says Derrick.

"How about you don't do that ever?"

"No promises."

Soon after, a nearby banging door snaps Jayson's attention away from the hotdogs.

Across the rocky and clumpy sand, Lexia exits a rundown concrete cube marked as a public bathroom. She is carrying an urban camouflage backpack with one hand, and her other hand rakes through her thick white hair with showmanship flare and perched on her head is an umbrella hat.

Jayson's moisture disappears in his mouth and the blood in his brain drains as Lexia saunters her way over.

Lexia's bikini is a tantalizing shade of pink, and clings tightly to her body. A choker sits above her two-toned neck fluff, attached to the bikini top by bronze chains. The pink top accentuates the swell of her white furred breasts, and fully exposes her flat stomach, covered in white and flanked with brown fur. The skimpy pink bottom linked together by bronze chains hugs her hips, exposing the brown fur covering her toned muscles. She's slipped into flipflops that snugly cradle her white and brown feet, and her hips have a sway to them as her toned, white-furred legs carry her forward.

Jayson's pulse quickens, his heart thumps heavily like a drum in his chest, as his gaze traces the contours of her muscular physique. He is so used to seeing Lexia wearing her homemade armor that he didn't realize how her body isn't merely strong; it is chiseled to perfection, each curve and color working hand in hand as an indisputable testament to her physical might and beauty. His eyes and brain burn at the sight of an unstoppable tempest of desire, wrapped in an irresistibly ferocious body.

And for that moment of staring and sudden mental poetry, Jayson's brain does not register that Derrick is staring at him with an odd look while Lexia has finally made her way to him.

Jayson only snaps back to reality when Lexia drops her backpack next to his feet.

"Enjoying the view?" teases Lexia.

Jayson averts his gaze as he straightens up, trying to shake off the unexpected lust that had ambushed him.

"Nope," says Jayson.

Lexia chuckles. "Sure, you aren't. Your brain totally didn't break when you saw me coming over."

"Hey, everyone's going to stare at a lady who dresses like a stripper," says Jayson.

"Then why don't you slip me a buck? There's a few spots you can use."

Jayson wrinkles his nose and turns his body away from Lexia so she can't see his hot face.

"Lexia, what the hell are you wearing? I said reservoir, not the mayor's pool party," says Derrick.

"It's my bikini," says Lexia as she adjusts her umbrella hat. "I got it off the clearance rack from Vicky's Secret."

"I can tell," says Jayson.

"Shut it," growls Lexia, pointing at him. "I saw you drooling."

Jayson shrugs with a small smirk. Then his ears perk, and he leaps out of his seat and claws at the ground, flinging clumpy dirt and pebbles all around. He finishes with a triumphant yell and holds up an old bike chain for Lexia and Derrick to see.

"Ha! This will get me a penny!" says Jayson.

Derrick and Lexia stare at Jayson, their silence amplified by the sizzling hotdogs and the waves lapping at the sandy shores.

Seconds pass and Lexia takes a deep breath and looks at Derrick. "I'm going to swim now."

Lexia tosses her umbrella hat on the table and runs off, passing Jayson. The Hobo looks over his shoulder to watch her splash in the water and then dive in. She pops up a few seconds later, gasping for air and brushing her bangs away from her brown eyes, teeth chattering and body trembling.

"The water's cold!" yells Lexia.

Derrick goes back to lazily turning the hotdogs. "Yep, that's generally how water is. Jayson, you should join her. You need a bath, anyway."

"Nope," says Jayson swiftly. He hurries to a tree and pulls out bike wheel spokes from the thistles surrounding it. "I've got metal to find!"

Derrick frowns. "Right..."

"Oh, more cans!" Jayson runs to a graffiti-tagged rock with his bag and starts collecting a cluster of old beer cans and bean cans tossed around the area.

"Oh, sweet! Bike handlebars!" says Jayson a few seconds later. "I'm going to have a bike in no time!"

The sound of Derrick sighing mingles with the faint splash of Lexia enjoying her swim, and the clink of Jayson adding to his haul. When Jayson finishes stuffing his bag, he giggles madly and dives into a bush, tossing out more old beer cans, and Derrick shakes his head while turning a hotdog consumed with flames.

"He's getting dunked," grumbles Derrick.

"Oh, more junk!" yells Jayson excitedly, his voice echoing as he runs further into the trees.

(((ooo)))

Several minutes later, Jayson makes his way back to the picnic site. His fully stuffed bag jingles with metallic chatter as he hops along the chunky sand and gnarled plants of the Bliss Town Reservoir. He lugs his collection back to the table with a smile on his dirty face, but when he arrives, he doesn't see Derrick anywhere. New hotdogs are on the grill, while the black and shriveled ones are on paper plates covered in napkins and weighed down with rocks.

He drops his bag by the picnic table and looks around again. There is no sign of Derrick anywhere, and Lexia is swimming in circles, lost in her own world. After some seconds of pacing, Jayson stops and scratches his dirty hair, breaking some caked-on mixture of grease and dandruff.

Then his ears twitch at the sound of branches rustling. Suddenly a shadow descends upon him. He looks up, and before he can react, he is yanked off his feet and held firmly by talons. The world zooms away, and everything tilts as he is released in midair.

Jayson screams and flails his limbs, trying to grab anything hidden in the air to stop his fall.

Vertigo slams into him as airborne became waterborne with a splash that swallows his screams and curses. When Jayson breaks the surface seconds later, he gasps for air and sputters, kicking and beating the cold water wildly while Lexia bobs next to him with a smirk cresting her wet features.

"Damn it, Derrick!" yells Jayson.

"*Bath time...*" teases Lexia with a sing-song tone.

Jayson growls and slams his palm into the water, splashing Lexia's face. She gasps and splashes him back. Jayson splashes harder and faster, and Lexia returns the assault. All the while, Derrick lands next to his grill and lights another cigarette with a small smile on his beak.

During the altercation, Lexia pushes herself forward and rams into Jayson, knocking his footing off the mud. He slips backwards, grabbing Lexia's arm, and both scream as they are submerged.

The pair thrashes around underwater, and then bursts out, gasping for air. Just for Lexia to wrap her arms around Jayson, pinning his arms to his sides. She picks him up and slams him back in the water, taking herself with him.

They pop up a moment later, and with them is a brief moment of shared laughter. And back at the grill, Derrick smiles and puts more burnt hotdogs on a paper plate.

Bliss Town Reservoir- 04

"Oh my gosh, this place sucks!" cries Mortimer, his eyes wide and pulsing from disappointment-induced rage as he and Claribel stare at the sorry state of the Bliss Town Reservoir, both dressed casually.

Mortimer is wearing jeans and a dark-colored shirt with swimming sharks stitched on it. In his grip are a pair of coolers, and a pistol is holstered on his hip, and his raccoon mask covers his burnt face.

Claribel is wearing a button-up long-sleeve shirt decorated with *Block World* bricks of various colors, airy pants, and her Stetson is snug on her head. Slung on her back is her rifle and she is clutching a large beach umbrella in one hand and a basket of beach towels in another. She too is staring at the sorry scene with wide eyes.

Mortimer and Claribel cautiously approach the sandy shore from their position in the parking lot, their steps crunching on gravel and discarded debris along the way. The state of the reservoir really is miserable; plastic bottles, greasy paper, cans of various uses, other nasty things, all manner of neglect laid bare.

"They don't even try to keep it clean," says Claribel.

"Well, you know what? I don't want to walk around through this sorry excuse of a reservoir all day looking for a spot that isn't covered in garbage," says Mortimer. He looks around and spots a tree with a grill and picnic table underneath its canopy. All of it is covered in trash and graffiti, but he points at it with a determined glint in his eyes. "There! We'll clean that spot and call dibs!"

Mortimer runs ahead, rips weeds away from a public trash can, and starts picking up the trash while Claribel works on clearing up the sand to make a good spot to lay the towels and umbrella. While they work, they hear laughter and splashing nearby, but they are too focused on their work to peek at the people having fun.

When Claribel is done, she sets rocks on the corners of the towels to keep the cool breeze from blowing them away, and she stabs the umbrella in the ground and pops it open. She looks around and sees a nearby block-shaped concrete structure labeled as a bathroom.

"I'm going to change," says Claribel.

"Sure thing," says Mortimer, chucking more trash into the overflowing trash can.

It doesn't take long for Claribel to reach the bathroom, and when she opens the door, she finds that the interior has a green tint, lights flicker and hum, and graffiti of various natures are scribbled everywhere. There's even a chunky brown hand print streaking down the wall near a stall with an "out of order" sign taped to it. Her tongue flicks out and is immediately desecrated with the toxic scent of bleach, urine, feces, and other things she can't place.

Claribel coughs and gags and slams the door shut, shuddering and tail rattling as she desperately sucks in somewhat clean air. After she takes a long, deep, raspy breath, she marches towards a large bush.

"Forget this. I'm changing outside," says Claribel.

****

Back at the site, Mortimer is shoving weeds and branches into the public grill. He quickly changed into his wetsuit when Claribel left, putting him in a pale gray masterpiece with white shark teeth inside its dark gray bands, and reflective neon yellow bands on his shoulders, hips, and back.

His tail flicks in aggravation as he continues shoving as much as he can into the slender rectangle that makes the grill. His irritation is contrasted by the calming waves brushing against the sandy shores, and the shouts and splashing nearby.

Footsteps approach Mortimer, and then Claribel clears her throat.

Mortimer turns around and his ears perk and body stiffens at the beautiful sight before him.

Claribel's figure is encased in a vibrant cobalt wetsuit, the dark sapphire bands perfectly accentuating her curves. The collar, adorned with an array of seashells, nestles against her throat. The suit clings to her, molding itself around every dip and swell of her body like a second skin. It traces the contour of her hips, hugs the curves of her breasts, and slithers down her thighs with an audacious intimacy that makes Mortimer's mouth water.

"What do you think?" asks Claribel sheepishly.

Mortimer tugs at his wetsuit collar, his pulse beating rapidly and his throat bobbing from swallowing the drool pooling in his mouth.

"Eh… I think it looks…"

Mortimer's voice trails off and Claribel cringes and rubs her hands together.

"It's bad, isn't it?" says Claribel.

"No! You look better than me or anyone else out here!" blurts Mortimer. "You're like a star surfer or a professional swimmer. The kinds that go on cereal boxes."

"Are you sure?"

"Yes, I'm sure. Now, why don't you relax while I get some food cooking."

Claribel nods, clamps her hands together, and sits on her beach towel, which is also decorated with seashells. She watches the water, and Mortimer rubs his hands eagerly after he puts his cooler on the table.

"Alright, now for the beginning of the good part," says Mortimer. He lifts the lid, and slams it shut. "Never mind!"

Claribel looks at Mortimer. "What?"

"I forgot the hotdogs!"

"What!" Claribel opens the cooler and sees condiments, from mayo, to mustard, to relish, and whole wheat buns, but not hotdogs. She closes the lid and looks at Mortimer with wide eyes and a slack jaw. "How'd you forget the hotdogs?"

"I don't know how I forgot the hotdogs! They're probably still on the dining room table, no doubt being devoured by those One-O fanatics."

****

At the safehouse, Dacre goes into the kitchen and stops dead in his tracks when he sees a tower of ten red and yellow hotdog packets on the table.

"Hey, Rolland?" calls Dacre without looking away from the hotdogs.

"What?" says Rolland from the living room.

"What's with all the hotdogs?"

"Don't know, don't care. Shae dropped a blue reverse, so it's your turn again."

Dacre stares at the hotdog stack for another couple of seconds before he shrugs, snatches a packet, and walks back to the living room.

****

At the reservoir, Claribel sits at the picnic table and rests her chin on her folded arms.

"I guess we're going to have to go to the store, unless you want to drink mustard and eat relish," says Claribel.

Mortimer lays his arms and head on the cooler, groaning. "Dang it, this..."

His voice trails off as the scent of burnt hotdogs floats into his nose, and Claribel's forked tongue flicks out. She scrunches her brows and licks the air again while Mortimer's nose twitches from his sniffing.

Their brains register the delicious sent, and they look at each other with bright smiles and say, "Hotdogs!"

Bliss Town Reservoir- 05

Jayson collapses on the reservoir's sand, limbs burning and water pouring out of his heavy clothes. Mud clings to him, and the water carrying the grease in his hair streaks down his face.

A shadow descends upon him, and he looks over his shoulder and sees Lexia grinning at him maniacally and rubbing her hands together with the sunlight shining on her back. Water traces and drips off of her in all the right places. Jayson tries crawling, fighting the urges that Lexia the Succubus is imposing on his mind.

"You're still dirty, Jayson. Time for more super-duper pampering!" says Lexia.

"I don't need any more pampering!" says Jayson.

Lexia grabs Jayson's legs, and with a mighty heave, she throws him back into the reservoir. His scream is short-lived as he lands face first on the water, and then Lexia jumps on his back pushing him further in.

Jayson thrashes and twists and when he pops out of the water, sputtering and gagging, Lexia wraps her arms around him. She drags him to the shallow portion of the reservoir, pressing his back against her chest. Once in the shallow end, she sits down, wraps her legs around Jayson, and starts scrubbing her fingers in his hair, breaking the clumps of mud, grease, and dandruff that paste his brown hair into tangled knots.

"Derrick, are you going to let Lexia do this to me!" yells Jayson.

"You need a bath," says Derrick.

"I took a shower at the gym a few days ago!"

"And how long is a few days ago?" says Lexia, grimacing when she looks at dead bugs and hair strands stuck to her fingers.

"A few days ago, is a few days ago," says Jayson.

Jayson struggles some more, but suddenly stops when his ears pick up a familiar voice, and he catches movement out of the corner of his eye. He turns his head, and his eyes bulge.

The Fixers are walking towards their camp, with a rifle on the snake's back and a pistol on the fox's hip. And they're both wearing form-fitting wetsuits that do an excellent job of showcasing their peak physiques.

"Uh, Lexia," says Jayson.

"What?" says Lexia, still scrubbing his hair.

"The Fixers are here."

Lexia snaps her head to where Jayson is looking, and then she hops up, shoving Jayson back in the water.

"Derrick, look out!" yells Lexia.

Jayson pops out of the water, coughing and wheezing, and when he wipes the water from his eyes, he sees Lexia has her bazooka out. He doesn't bother trying to figure out where she kept that weapon. Instead, his focus is on the two Fixers heading towards them.

Meanwhile, Derrick looks up from his grill, and Mortimer and Claribel stop in their tracks. Both sides narrow their eyes, but Mortimer is the first to slowly raise his hands, while Derrick stretches his hand towards his rifle. Claribel has also unsung her rifle and is aiming it at Derrick.

"Easy now, I'm not here for trouble," says Mortimer. He looks at Lexia as she runs out of the water with Jayson following close behind, and he grins. "Nice..."

Claribel glares at him, and Lexia smiles brightly and runs her fingers through her dripping wet hair, striking a pose for optimal viewing pleasure.

"Thanks, handsome! I'm glad someone appreciates my assets," says Lexia.

Jayson stops next to Lexia, panting and holding her arm for support while thick globs of water drip off him. His other hand is gripping his wooden weapon's hilt.

"Lexia, please don't flirt with the guy trying to kill us," says Jayson, short of breath.

"I'm not here to kill anybody. I just want some hotdogs," says Mortimer.

"Ain't got any," says Derrick.

"You got a stack of hotdogs right there!" says Mortimer, pointing at the plate of burnt hotdogs.

"Them ain't hotdogs."

"You gaslighting tard, those are hotdogs!"

"They're burnt hotdogs."

Mortimer's eye twitches, and Claribel uses her tail to tug on Mortimer's tail, while Lexia inches closer with her bazooka at the ready.

"Mortimer let's go. You wanted to relax, remember?" says Claribel.

"Fine. I guess we'll go. And starve. Alone and unloved," says Mortimer.

"Don't be a crybaby," says Derrick.

"Wait! Everyone, just stop for a second!" yells Jayson.

Everyone looks at Jayson, and he has his hands raised towards both factions. He takes a deep breath and exhales slowly. When his thoughts are collected, he looks at Derrick, but still keeps his hands up as a call for peace between the two sides.

"Derrick, there's more than enough hotdogs to share," says Jayson.

"Jayson don't give food to the people trying to kill us," says Lexia.

Jayson wrinkles his nose at Lexia. "You were just flirting with the fox not too long ago.".

"The name's Mortimer," says Mortimer.

Jayson jabs his thumb towards Mortimer without looking away from Lexia. "Yeah, you were flirting with Morty."

Mortimer sneers, and Lexia gasps heavily while Derrick looks in his cooler.

"I was not flirting!" claims Lexia.

"You **were** flirting and trying to seduce him with your harlot attire," says Claribel.

"Can it, snake."

"Claribel."

"More like Clari-*lame*."

"Anyway!" blurts Jayson. "Derrick, being hungry sucks, and there's plenty of hotdogs to go around. They don't want any trouble today, and neither do we, so let's just call a temporary truce and enjoy the reservoir like what you wanted and what..."

Jayson's pointed finger shifts between the two Fixers. His voice drifts to silence, and Mortimer sighs and barely lifts his hand.

"I wanted to relax, too, but that doesn't seem to be happening," says Mortimer.

"Right, Morty wanted relaxation, too," says Jayson.

"Stop calling me Morty."

"Or what?"

"Or we'll call you *Jay*," threatens Claribel.

Both sides silently stare at Claribel, and she looks between them, keeping excellent trigger discipline while aiming her rifle at Derrick, who is now closing his cooler.

"What?" says Claribel.

"None of us are having hotdogs," says Derrick.

"You're being a real dick, you know that?" says Mortimer. "And I'm pretty sure you're the bird who shot me."

"I did shoot you, and I said none of us are having hotdogs because there ain't anything to put on them. There're no buns, no ketchup, no mustard. It'll be bland and that's nasty."

Now everyone looks at Derrick, and Lexia runs to his cooler, opens it, and then glares at him after slamming it shut.

"How did you forget the condiments!" says Lexia.

"Well, you're in luck," starts Mortimer.

"We don't need condiments," interrupts Jayson.

"Guys," says Mortimer.

"You need condiments for a hotdog. It's the law," says Lexia.

"Since when?" says Jayson.

Mortimer raises a finger. "Can I—"

"It ain't the law but it should be," says Derrick.

"I just want to say—" says Mortimer.

"That would put you on the wrong side of the law today. Plus, how is that law going to be enforced?" says Jayson.

"But it ain't the law, so I'm not breaking the law, but it should be law," says Derrick.

"Can everyone—" says Mortimer.

"It'll be a stupid, unenforceable law," says Jayson heatedly.

"At the very least it should be a de facto law. Like cafeteria segregation between jocks, nerds, goths, cheerleaders, and retards. Only with hotdogs," says Lexia.

"That ain't nice calling someone a retard, Lexia," says Derrick.

"Yeah, that's mean. Anyway, I have—" says Mortimer.

"So, would the no-condiments group go to the retard table or the goth table?" says Jayson.

"HEY!" yells Claribel, her booming voice echoing in the reservoir.

The group stops talking, and Mortimer rubs his ear while Claribel takes a deep breath.

"We have condiments," says Claribel.

Jayson, Lexia, and Derrick all vocalize their pleasant surprise and nod to each other.

"Now you tell us," says Derrick.

"Why didn't you say so?" says Lexia.

Claribel scowls and Mortimer sighs heavily and turns away.

"Whatever, I'm grabbing the condiments. Don't start without us," says Mortimer.

Bliss Town Reservoir- 06

Mortimer drops his cooler on the table, next to where Jayson is sitting. The fox flips open the lid with a triumphant smile and pulls out hotdog buns and a variety of condiments.

"Behold! Weiner sauces!" says Mortimer.

"Never say that again," says Derrick.

Jayson grabs a jar of relish and turns the container around, just to see it says, "Mark's Mayo."

Jayson gags and throws it perfectly in the trash, and while Mortimer continues arranging the condiments, Jayson checks the expiration dates. Claribel also arrives, carrying the umbrella and towels, and she drops them on the ground next to Lexia, who is laying on her stomach, wearing her umbrella hat, legs gently kicking the air as she stares at the boats moving around the reservoir.

"You do realize all these condiments have two or three days left on them," says Jayson, turning a mustard bottle in his hand.

"Oh yeah. I knew that," says Mortimer.

Jayson stares at Mortimer for a few seconds before his lips pucker and sets the mustard down. As this happens, Derrick puts the hotdogs in the buns, giving everyone four hotdogs. However, due to his overzealous love of burning hotdogs, the stack of burnt food is still on the large side. Meanwhile, Claribel lays on the towel next to Lexia and also stares at the water.

"So, how are you going to try to kill us today? Shoot? Stab? Poison?" asks Lexia.

"Today is my day off," replies Claribel.

"Fixers don't get day-offs."

"Yes, they do. I have guaranteed off days on Mondays, Wednesdays, and Fridays."

Lexia props herself on her elbow so she can look at Claribel with a raised brow. "Hold on, are you saying you're a part-time Fixer?"

"I am," says Claribel proudly.

"Hotdogs are done!" says Derrick.

Claribel immediately bolts to the picnic table, leaving Lexia blinking in confusion.

At the table, Jayson rubs his hands together, licking his lips while his nose tingles with the delicious scent of ketchup, mustard, and burnt hotdogs.

Mortimer sits down across from Jayson after passing out water bottles and is joined by Claribel soon after.

Lexia takes a seat next to Jayson, using her towel to shield her exposed thighs from potential splinters. Derrick sits next to Lexia soon after, and both sides stay quiet with their hands twitching in anticipation and their eyes drifting for signs of hostility.

Seconds tick by, and Jayson holds up his hotdog.

"Well, I'm tired of waiting," says Jayson. He takes a massive bite out of his food, chews, and nods. "Not bad."

That is when the others begin eating. At first, they are silent as they eat, but a couple of minutes later, Mortimer looks at Jayson, his mouth full of food.

"This is nice. I would say we should do this more often, but I'm going to kill you tomorrow," says Mortimer.

"Sure, you will," says Jayson with a smile.

"Were you a marksman by any chance?" asks Claribel to Derrick, nodding to his rifle.

"I enlisted to be a dishwasher," says Derrick.

Claribel scrunches her brows and Lexia turns her hotdog and inspects the sauce with a critical eye.

"This mustard tastes funny," says Lexia.

Nobody cares to answer her, so the conversations carry on while they eat, with the sounds of the waves brushing against the sand giving a calming background noise for them.

The hotdog piles shrink over time, and soon the two groups find themselves full. By that time, the sun dips below the reservoir's horizon, and they work together to clean up, placing their trash in the proper receptacle, and by that point Lexia is dry enough to put on some casual clothes to cover her swimwear.

"Those were the best burnt hotdogs I ever had," says Mortimer.

"Yeah, they were good, but I need to go now," says Jayson. He picks up his sack of scrap metal and slings it over his shoulder. "I should be able to make it to the scrap metal place before they close."

"I need to go, too. My mom is probably wondering where I am, and my part time job starts in a few hours," says Lexia as she folds up her towel.

Derrick nods. "Drive safe. Walk safe." He looks at Mortimer and Claribel. "You two stay here until we're long gone."

Mortimer stretches his arms and legs. "Fine by me. I still want to swim."

Derrick grunts, and Jayson and Lexia walk away from the reservoir. They are silent, and briefly see Derrick fly over their heads, and when they reach Lexia's car, they stop and look at the reservoir again.

From their spot, they can see Mortimer picking up Claribel, and despite her protests, Mortimer still runs and dives in the water, cackling and holding her tight. The Fixers' voices are drowned by the splashing, and they pop up a moment later with Claribel shouting angrily and Mortimer laughing again.

"Well, that was something else," says Jayson, turning his attention to Lexia.

"Yep," says Lexia.

"So, can I get a ride to the scrap metal place?"

Lexia looks at Jayson, and he smiles and bats his lashes.

"Please?" says Jayson.

Lexia huffs and opens the passenger door for him. "Fine."

"Thanks!"

Jayson tosses the scrap bag in the backseat and buckles up in the front passenger seat. Lexia gets in the driver's seat, starts the engine, and heavy metal plays through the speakers as she reverses out of her spot. Then they leave the reservoir in silence.

****

The sun is low in the sky, casting long shadows across Bliss Town, painting everything in hues of orange and red while the cracks in the sky warp everything near it.

Lexia's car pulls up to a block-shaped building with four large chimneys, thick walls, and razor wire fencing. A camera watches them, and when the vehicle stops in front of the entrance, Jayson unbuckles himself, grabs his bag, and goes to the driver's side door. Lexia rolls down her window and Jayson smiles at her.

"Thanks again for the ride. I can take it from here," says Jayson.

"Good. I'm outta here," says Lexia.

Immediately after, she reverses out of her spot and speeds away. Jayson sighs, shoulders his bag, and enters the building, passing a pair of vending machines along the way.

A bell dings, and bright light and a creaky fan assaults Jayson's senses. His footsteps echo in the bare room as he goes to the counter. Electric currents hum loudly, and Jayson leans over to see the female rabbit receptionist laying curled up in the corner, eyes wide and grinning broadly as she giggles to herself. Her eyes snap to him, and she contorts her body as she rolls on her feet, still giggling and shuddering with glazed and dilated eyes.

"Demon-angel, angel-demon, I see you. Do you see me?" says the receptionist.

"I'm just here to drop off some metal," says Jayson.

The receptionist gasps and her smile spreads wide. "You do see me! And you're made of butterflies!"

She holds her hands out to Jayson.

"Come see with me, butterflies!" says the receptionist.

Jayson frowns and steps back, clutching his bag tighter. But before anything terrible can happen, the side door opens, and Mariana Cross enters the lobby with a clipboard, wearing a thick, gray jumpsuit.

She grabs the receptionist by the arm and drags her away, completely silent, while the receptionist spews a stream of gibberish and cackles. The door she and the receptionist pass through slams shut, and Jayson blinks, his brain's gears grinding to process what he just witnessed.

Mariana returns a few seconds later, props a chair underneath the door's knob, keeping the receptionist locked in the room, and she goes to the counter. Jayson stares at her dumbly, and she stares back.

"What do you want?" says Mariana.

"I'm sorry, I thought you worked at Taco King and the movie theater," says Jayson.

"I do," says Mariana.

"Oh... Um, okay... I have metal I want to sell."

Jayson puts the bag on the counter, and Mariana stiffly grabs it and carries it to the backroom.

Jayson drums his fingers on the counter and looks around, hearing the faint giggles and mutters of the trapped receptionist.

A few seconds later, Mariana returns with a small stack of bills, a receipt, and the empty bag, and she gives them to Jayson.

"Five bucks," says Mariana.

Jayson snatches the money and rolls up his bag. "Thanks! I can get a value taco."

"You're banned from Taco King."

"Oh... Well, there's always the vending machines!"

"Don't use the C-Cola machine. It'll explode and kill you with a puncture wound to the neck," says Mariana.

Jayson stares at her, brows scrunched and lips tight, and Mariana returns his look with a bored expression. A tingle runs down Jayson's spine, and he slowly backs up and keeps his eyes on Mariana.

She doesn't blink.

Jayson opens the door and gives Mariana one last look before exiting the building. The cool night air is a stark difference to the early heatwave, but compared to inside, the outside world is warm.

A gentle wind blows dead leaves across the concrete pathway, and Jayson goes to the two vending machines near the entrance. He stops in front of the right vending machine, which advertises cold drinks from C-Cola. He puts his first bill against its money slot but stops.

He looks at the left vending machine, which has soda from P-Cola.

Jayson's eyes shift between the two machines. His nose and ears twitch, and he slowly shifts to the P-Cola machine, hesitates, and then inserts his money and selects a bottle of Grapetastic.

The vending machine hums and shakes, and whines with bright flashing lights and sparks. Jayson's eyes widen and he steps back. Then there is a pleasant ding and a ruckus as the bottle tumbles down.

When the bottle lands in the retrieval area, Jayson hesitates, and slowly reaches in while smoke rolls around him. He pulls out an ice-cold bottle of grape soda, which feels like a rock in his grip. Jayson sneers and looks at the bottle.

"Man, it's all shaken up," he says, adding with a heavy sigh, "Whatever. I'll just have to open it slowly."

Jayson walks away after that, wincing as he cautiously opens the bottle to barely release its pressure. And off in the distance, too far for Jayson to see, is Trafford Augustine. He is on a roof with binoculars and a stash of protein bars, protein shake mixes, bottles of water, and a thirty-six-pack of classic C-Cola soda cans.

As Trafford watches Jayson walk down the sidewalk, shaking his hand to flick off the grape soda that bubbled out, his cellphone rings. He swiftly answers it without taking his eyes off the Hobo.

"Trafford Augustine speaking," he says.

"*Status,*" says Mr. Exe.

"We've got a goldmine of data over the past few days. Surprisingly, nobody tried killing each other today, so that was odd, but welcoming."

"*Can we use the subjects?*"

"Definitely. And there's something odd about Lexia Hartwick and Derrick Marlow. I'm going to need to see if we have files on them. And the fox and snake, Mortimer Walters and Claribel Belle Blair, also seem to be an odd bunch. I'm also going to need information on them if we have any."

"*Done. Check your email when you return to your office.*"

Trafford smiles. "Thanks, boss."

"Keep me updated."

Mr. Exe hangs up, and Trafford returns his phone to his pocket, still keeping his eyes on Jayson. His smile grows as he grabs a massive protein bar with his free hand and tears off the wrapper with his teeth. Then he chomps down half off it and giggles and shudders.

"Keep walking, Hobo. Enjoy the days while you can, because I promise you and your friends, the worst is yet to come."